viktor demoskev

Defense

3

dedication

For those who are,
and always will be...
VEGAS STRONG.

1
life trouble

Scarlett

Well, I'll be damned. Georg Kolochev just scored the first goal in game seven. Pretty impressive for a solid defenseman. Of course, that dude's on top of the world. He just got engaged a few days ago and won the Norris Trophy earlier tonight, so who knows what the rest of this game holds for him. He's having the time of his friggin' charmed life out there.

I came in through the back entrance today because the hype is real. As in: *Las Vegas comes out for its team.* On any regular season game day, that's the standard around here. But throw in the Stanley Cup Finals, game seven, winner takes all?

Yeah, the Crush fans are very "extra" tonight.

There was a stage set up out front, with a performance by some Vegas-based rapper that I've never heard of. There's a drum line of kids from a local high school, with banners and balloons everywhere. The marketing team hired a crew of good-looking college kids to shoot T-shirts out of cannons at the crowd. They even set up a big video screen outside, so people could watch the game if they didn't have tickets.

In my lowly position as a media coordinator for the Crush, I mostly write press releases, send them out, and then make follow-up calls to reporters. I like it okay. It's a job that didn't require a college degree, just writing skills and a bulldog's determination. I've got both of those.

Before this job, I filled in for Holly Laurent—sorry, Holly Kazmeirowicz; Holly Laurent-Kazmeirowicz?   Holly-Married-to-the-Hottest-Guy-Ever?—while she was out on maternity leave. Holly is our social media manager and *she is a genius.*

I thought I could top her performance while she was out, but I learned otherwise. Holly has a vision, and she knows how to execute it. Some people are just talented like that.

Me? I'm just trying to make it from point A to point B, wherever point B is. Hopefully, it's not anywhere near my second job, where I'm a cocktail server at the Tangiers casino. Hopefully, it's also not anywhere near the World Series of Poker...or the mafia. Both of those have caused my life trouble. No, let's shouty caps that and call it like it is. LIFE TROUBLE.

Right now, the "in-between" is in the owner's suite for game seven of the Stanley Cup finals with the Crush fighting to retain their championship status for a second year. My boss, Fiona, is up here, as well as my coworkers Holly and Daisy. Daisy is a shy, quiet sort. She embarrasses easily, as was evidenced when her dumbass ex-boyfriend sent like eleventy million flowers to the office and called as many times. He wanted her back even though she was done with him just on principle, and for embarrassing her at work.

My boss, Fiona, is married to some corporate type who works in Los Angeles. I think it's a loveless marriage and I doubt she sees him very often. She probably has some boy-toy-side-action, but who knows. Actually, I doubt it since she acts so uptight. She probably hasn't been laid in a long time.

It's exciting to be in the suite. I feel out of place with all these smart, rich people, but it's still fun to be up here, seeing the game from a place of privilege.

"Hey there," Pam says, nudging my shoulder with hers. Pam's a physical therapist for the Crush as well as the newly minted fiancée of hockey god, Georg Kolochev. She's got a celebratory glass of champagne in one hand and her phone in the other, as she takes photos of the game below. She's probably just having her break because she's dressed in her work attire, on call in the therapy room for players who need attention during the game.

"Hey. Congrats again to the two of you. That proposal the other night, though."

"Go big or go home," she says with a shrug and a mischievous grin.

"Well, you went big. And he's probably big, so..."

Pam snorts. "Way to go for the obvious, Scarlett."

"So, he is big, then? Asking for a friend, of course. For clinical and research purposes only."

Pam rolls her eyes and sticks out her tongue. She still looks pretty, even when she makes stupid faces. "I will not be sharing information about Georg's big dick—umm, I mean his *endowments* with anyone." She grins wickedly at first but then her expression takes on a wistful quality. I don't need to guess what she's thinking about right now. The big stick Georg is packing in his hockey pants.

"I want one of my own," I whine. "You've got Georg. Holly's got Evan. Where's my muscular, hot, well-endowed, hockey-playing Prince Charming?"

"No go with the nerd boys from the bar?" she asks, referencing our bar-fly night a while back.

"Oh, geesh, no. I don't even know why I gave them my number. They're from, like Ohio or something, in Vegas for a tech convention. I'd have more luck on Tinder."

"Wait, you're *not* on Tinder?" Pam's eyes go wide. "Scarlett Woods, you have truly shocked me."

"Very funny, girlie. I had it, but it's really just for booty calls. The dick pics got gross real fast."

"You're so young, I'd think you'd just want to get out there and play for now. Why the rush to find everlasting love?"

I shrug and look out at the crowd, the ice. Anything to avoid crying. "I don't know. I just…" She's right, I am young—in years. I don't feel young though. I feel old and jaded from certain life experiences I never want to repeat as long as I'm on this earth.

Pam's voice softens before she lays the big question on me. "I know you were in a relationship not too long ago, right?"

"I was…I-I don't talk about Stephen much. He was a pro-poker player. His life was in the games. He, um, committed suicide. We think."

"You think?"

I nod, an errant tear escaping. I wipe it away with the back of my hand. "It was really weird and suspicious. But that's pretty much the story of my life."

"Weird *and* suspicious?"

"Yeah." I take a big breath in and then let it out slowly. "Growing up in Vegas has been a wild ride."

"You should write a book someday, my friend," she says with a gentle smile and a quick hug. "And on that note, my break is over. See you after the game? We can talk some more if you want."

"Maybe, yeah." I smile and send her on her way.

After Pam is out of the suite, I look over my shoulder and see a cute guy by the buffet table and decide to do something about it. *Scarlett, you're gonna go flirt with that cute guy over there and make yourself feel better.*

I am so ready to get away from thoughts of Stephen, or the need to talk about him, or his gambling, or his death. He's the whole reason I took this job with the Crush, so I guess that's a good thing. I like hockey a lot, and it's been a decent, low-drama position. Exactly what I need out of a job that was meant to help me save up to pay off some debts from the past. Sucks to have obscene debts at the ripe old age of twenty-two, but that's right where I've landed in the scheme of things.

As I approach the buffet, the cute guy gives me a smile. A good start. I smile back and ask, "Enjoying the series so far?"

I grab a plate as he affirms that he is enjoying the series. Turns out his name is Leo and he's Max Terry's son. Which means he's rich and educated and sophisticated…and totally out of my league.

"Do you come to many games?" I ask as we nosh at a highboy table near the bar.

"No, I live in New York, so I just come for big games, or I watch when the team plays closer to home."

"Did you watch the game last season in New York, when Evan Kazmeirowicz got hammered by Viktor Demoskev?"

"I did see that game," he confirms. "My fiancée now refuses to watch Crush games because she hates that guy so much."

His fiancée. He said that on purpose. *Whomp,*

whomp. At least he's loyal to her. That's something at least.

"A lot of people sort of hate him. But honestly, he seems to have it together this season. The guys all get along pretty well now." I leave out the part about being inappropriately attracted to the big Russian defenseman. One, there's a strict no-fraternization policy for employees of the Crush and players on the team. Two, I've never even met Viktor Demoskev. I strictly admire from afar. I may let my mind whirl with inappropriate thoughts on occasion, but I've made sure to follow the rules.

"That's good," Leo says. "They make a formidable first line."

I nod and decide it's time to not make it awkward. "Well, nice meeting you, Leo. Enjoy the rest of the game."

He nods. "You too…Rosie?"

"Scarlett." *I think I'm just gonna…go…now.*

With my cheeks probably a match for my hair, I turn toward the exit, only to find Holly coming through it holding a crying baby. Her baby, of course.

"Hey Scarlett, thank God you're here." She looks like she could use a hand—and possibly a stiff drink.

"What can I do to help?" I'd love to have something useful to do other than feel out of place in the owner's suite. Hobnobbing is just not in my skill set.

"Pam is working during the break between periods

and I'd like to include it in the postings. Unfortunately, Dany is super fussy, so I need to change and feed her. Can you round up a photographer and get down there to do some captions and photos for social media?"

"I would love to."

"Really?" she asks, looking relieved but still a little unsure. "I know it's way more fun to be up here. I wouldn't ask if..."

"No, it's cool. I'd much rather have something useful to do."

"You're a lifesaver and I could kiss you right now. I think we're at a stage when I'm going to have to get someone to watch her during games."

"I don't think anyone minds her being here," I say, trying to distract the baby with a silly boo-boo face. "Max Terry sure turns into a pile of mush around her. And you, for that matter."

She blushes. Kind of normal for her. "He's been really sweet to us all," she says. "Okay, so I'll just let Sid Lane know to meet you down in the locker rooms."

I give a thumbs-up and make my way to the door. The arena is kind of a maze, and I still get a little turned around sometimes, especially when heading to areas where I don't spend a lot of time. The locker rooms would be included on this list. I think I've been in there twice. I need to go down three levels to the main level and then take a service elevator down another level. I go the wrong way off the elevator, of course, and end up walking all the way around the circle like a big dummy.

Sid Lane, team photographer, waits for me in the hallway. He's young looking, with rosy cheeks and messy, dark hair. His eyes are bright blue. He's cute, if a little on the scrawny side.

"Heyyyy Sid," I greet him, batting my eyes and being purposely silly and flirtatious. "How's life today?"

"Livin' the dream, Scarlett."

He always says that, by the way. He's either hopelessly optimistic or darkly sarcastic. I can't tell.

"We're supposed to get therapy pics and captions for Holly's social media?"

"That's the marching order," he says. "There's a coaching review going on, but once they finish, we can go in."

"Perfect," I say, just as the door opens.

And what do you know…

The first thing to meet my eyes is my "inappropriate attraction" stretched out on a therapy table being worked over by Pam.

I give myself a mental shake and put on my professional mask, reminding my libido I'm here to do a job. A task that absolutely does not include ogling Viktor Demoskev.

I tell myself that. I really do.

But I don't listen very well, because I find myself wishing those were my hands on his body instead of Pam's.

2

the mad russian

Viktor

"**M**y fucking hamstring is tied in knots," I growl.

"Cramp or injury?" Pamela, the blonde therapist asks.

"Cramp."

"All right," Dale, the trainer says. "Let's have Pam do a deep-tissue massage and then you and I can do some stretching."

I lie face down on the table as Pamela starts to work on my leg. "*Xyecoc*," I snarl. *Cocksucker.* That hurt. "Sorry, Pamela."

"I've heard worse," she says with a laugh. "I owe you a little bit of pain anyway, though, don't I?"

I push my lips out, somewhat annoyed. I accidentally knocked her to the ground in a stupid bar brawl with Georg and Evan a season ago. I feel badly because I was a certifiable asshole that night.

She seems satisfied with how things resolved though. I know her little comment is meant in jest. But I find my sense of humor lacking now, so I don't respond.

"How is that?" She thankfully lets the topic drop.

"It is good. You found the spot."

She and Dale talk about another player's injury as I think on Coach Brown's feedback. He seems pleased with my play. Georg Kolochev and I could not be more different as defensive players. Tyler Lockhardt, as well. Where Georg is loose and cocky with a wide-angle eye for the field of play, Tyler is tight and aggressive. He plays to fight. There is talent there, for sure, but he has probably spent more time in the penalty box than anyone else on the team this year. That's not a compliment, though he certainly views it as a badge of honor. Me? I'm a brick wall. I am built to stop players from getting too close to the goal. That is all.

Suddenly, I am pulled from my thoughts, distracted by a guy with a camera. He takes a photo, and I scowl.

"For social media," the red-headed beauty beside him explains. "Holly sent us down."

"No one wants a picture taken when injured," I snap.

"Well, it's a hard-fought battle. People want to see what happens behind closed doors. What our players go through," she responds unapologetically.

I turn my head away from them.

"Don't worry about him," Pamela says. "He's cranky right now, but I think he's a big softie on the inside."

"That can be my caption."

I turn back toward her again. "It cannot be your caption," I protest.

She winks back at me in response and I take notice. It's strange because it doesn't happen very often. But this...this is a very attractive young woman. Long, silky red hair, shiny, with the ends curling at her tailbone. Bright green eyes and pale skin. A curvy body with a tiny waist and an ass my hands would enjoy meeting. What I would guess are a lush set of tits from the look of things. I wouldn't turn down the chance to verify that fact, either.

Suddenly, the pain at my hamstring takes a back seat to my consideration of this lovely rocket. A "rocket" being hockey slang for a very attractive female. And with all that long, pretty, red hair? I won't be able to think of her as anything other than the *Red Rocket* from here on out.

"Hey, Mad Russian," Evan, the team captain, interrupts my thoughts. "Move your mind off young Scarlett, there, and get up off the bench. Dale needs to stretch you out. We've got to head back out in a few."

I snarl at him in response, followed with a string of cursing in my native tongue. This makes Pamela laugh as I push myself up, swinging my legs over the side of the table. "Mad Russian" has been my nickname since I entered the NHL three years ago. I don't care for it, but I suppose it does fit my image well enough. I use it to my advantage on the ice to intimidate opposing players whenever an opportunity presents.

"I'm more than a little familiar with those words," she says, clapping me on the back. "That better?"

"It is, thank you, Pamela. You are very skilled."

"My pleasure, and this is Scarlett, by the way."

Scarlett is biting the corner of her bottom lip. Trying to hide a grin, I suppose. I hold out my hand. "Viktor." I find her handshake surprisingly firm for such small hands.

"Nice to meet you, Viktor. I work on Fiona's media team."

"That was my assumption."

"Be nice, asshole," Georg says as he passes by.

Pamela giggles and blows him a kiss. He skitters over and quickly pulls her in for a hot kiss. So hot that the coach yells for him to simmer down or sit on the bench.

He leaves as quickly as he arrived, off to consult with Evan on the second period plan.

"I apologize, Scarlett, I don't mean to be rude."

She shakes her head. "No worries. It was good meeting you, Viktor."

And then she's gone, going with the photographer to take pictures of other players. I stand, my eyes still on her as Dale leads me through stretches meant to loosen my hamstring further.

Finally feeling less cramped, I pull my skates back on as the team lines up to go back out. Tyler elbows me. "Got a little redhead on your mind, big guy?"

"No," I say, my face set into a frown.

"Liar." He grins at me like an idiot. "Fucking liar, liar, with your fucking pants on fire. I know a horny, lustful gaze when I see one."

"Yes, because you have it on your face every time you see Georg Kolochev," I answer drily.

"Har har." He rolls his eyes. "More like you see it every time I walk out and see the bunnies lined up to be plucked and fucked."

We head out so, thankfully, the conversation ends there. Though Tyler isn't kidding. Women, usually scantily clad, do line up outside to get our autographs and photos after every game. Some do get picked from the crowd by players who like random hookups. I very rarely partake lately. I've not been interested, so I mostly avoid the line. It adds to my reputation for being the "Mad Russian" asshole, I suppose, as I also do not sign autographs. But I don't care. I came here to play hockey, not be a celebrity.

I manage one last glance back at the beautiful red rocket, who is now laughing easily with Pamela and the photographer. I want to punch him for standing so close to her. This is stupid, right? I don't know her. Don't have any sort of claim over her. Yet I find I am so very attracted. An unexpected conundrum…

I'm still thinking of her as we make our way to the ice. But as soon as the roar of the crowd fills my ears, my head is back in the game. My only goal now is to help this team win, to be a championship team.

This is my only focus. *To win.*

3
he's going to score

Scarlett

Sid and I hook his camera to a slim laptop that he carries with him wherever he goes. He has a hard-shell backpack where he keeps his mobile photography and editing equipment. It looks like a little turtle shell.

We choose a handful of photos and he does some quick edits while I write captions. We send everything to Holly's phone so she can post to our various accounts. I find myself licking my lips a little at the images of Viktor Demoskev. He's wide-shouldered, muscular, and big. Just a really big dude. It looked impossible that Pam's portable therapy table could have held up the mass of him. It wasn't the first time I'd thought that too, but that man had looked like a giant, especially under Pam's small hands.

In the pictures, he's scowling. Of course, I guess that's kind of par for the course. He's clean-cut, no visible tattoos, short hair, and miles of muscles. He's a good-looking man, attractive, a sharp dresser, but not really a *nice*-looking man, if you know what I mean. He's got a brutal reputation, especially before he came to play for the Crush. He was not above hurting people—on the ice and occasionally even off it. They don't call him the Mad Russian for nothing. He earned that name.

Sid heads toward the ice as we finish up, and I go back up to the owner's suite to find Holly furiously working on her iPad. She looks up and smiles.

"These shots are great. And the captions are pretty funny, too."

"Thanks. It was kind of a funny scene down there. Those guys are—"

"Ugh," she groans, rolling her eyes. "You don't have to say another word. They're a bunch of goofballs."

"That's one word for it."

"Have a seat," she says, eyes back on the screen. "I'll probably send you back down for the second break to do it all again, if you don't mind?"

"No problem." I take the seat next to her.

She works as the baby sleeps against her chest. I'm not the biggest fan of babies. Or kids in general, really. But this is a cute sight. Holly's not that much older than me, twenty-five, but there's a maternal quality about her, a serenity that I don't know if I'll ever possess. And she's handling being a mom *and* a rock star social media manager better than I ever could.

I suppose I'm a little jealous of her. I felt quite competitive toward her when I was first given the interim role while she was out. I wanted to outdo her. Now, I guess I wish I could be more like her. Not with a baby, of course, but just as good at what I do, settled with a hot guy, looking like nothing fazes me.

Fat chance.

We're about seven minutes into the second period when a missed opportunity by the opposing team leaves Viktor Demoskev with nothing between him and the goal. He's careful not to take a shot too early, as we don't need an icing call right now, but he's only got a brief window in the confusion, so he hauls ass down the line.

"Watch this," I say, kind of to Holly but also just to myself. "He's going to score. The goalie's not even looking at him."

Holly's head pops up. "Who?" Her focus is on the ice, and she watches the play unfold. "Oh!"

And sure enough, Viktor takes a shot straight into the back of the net. It's a clean goal, one that absolutely no one, probably including Viktor himself, was expecting.

The sound in the owner's suite is deafening, so I can only imagine how loud it must be in the arena seats. People are going nuts, especially our players, who are jumping on Viktor's back on the ice.

Up two-nothing, the energy is high here in Crush command center. Fiona, our boss, takes a seat to my right.

"Two defensive goals in one game. Who'd have thought it?" she comments.

Fiona's hair is in a sharp, chin-length bob. She has straight-cut bangs and wears funky eyeglasses that match her well-tailored, Crush-colored dress. She's totally corporate and usually uptight. She's not a bad boss or anything and she sure knows what she's doing, but she still makes me feel uncomfortable.

Case in point. "Yeah, crazy," is my lame response.

"I'd like to try to draft up some pitches next week —features on the defensive team—Georg and Viktor specifically. Put it on your mental list of things to do?"

"Sure thing, boss."

"Great," she says. "And thanks for getting those captions for social today. They were really funny."

Even Holly looks up at this, her eyes narrowly scrutinizing our boss, who literally never compliments anyone. She's very particular and often very critical of our work. And silence usually means acceptance. It's weird to get a compliment.

"Um, no problem," I say. "Holly said the same."

"Well, she's done some comedic stuff before also, and it's worked really well."

Fiona sits for only another few minutes, awkwardly, before patting the arm of the chair and muttering something about checking in with Max on the post-game press event.

Holly waits for her to be out of earshot before saying, "She is really weird sometimes."

"You're not wrong about that," I agree. "We need to get her to take a weekend here and there so she can get some. I think she only sees her husband once a month."

"Yeah, you might be right. They're both workaholics," Holly says, focusing back on her work. "I know that sounds funny coming from me, but they're a whole other level."

"Have you met him? Her husband?" I ask.

"I met him," she answers, shrugging. "He's a slick dude. Handsome, well dressed. Gives you those smiles that make you feel naked. And not in a good way."

"Yuck," I say. "No wonder she's so unhappy."

"Who knows," Holly says. "I try not to assume what does or doesn't make other people happy. It usually leads to problems."

I'm about to dig for gossip, feeling there's more to Holly's statement than she's letting on, but we're interrupted by a very happy and maybe slightly tipsy Max Terry. He plops down to Holly's left and pulls her to him in a sloppy side-hug.

"I feel a win coming on," Max announces. "I've got my lucky charms. You and Evan started it. Love makes for a better player. I know it. And now Georg and Pam. And he's scored two goals in the series. I couldn't be happier."

"Yep," Holly says. "The defensive scoring in this game is giving me a lot of good social media fodder."

"Always working," Max says. "You should put that technology down and experience the game."

"Oh, but then I wouldn't retain my title as the best in the business, would I?" she asks wryly.

"Well, if you're not the best in the business, then I don't have to fight off other employers to keep you," Max counters, grinning.

Pam wanders in, having been in the stands for part of the period. She's got a plate of food and sits in the seat that Fiona just vacated. "Just shoving some food in my mouth before periods break," she says. "I can't believe this game."

"Yep, pretty crazy. Kinda like the high-end marriage proposal before the last game."

"Ha," she says. "Yes. But I wouldn't be me, if the proposal wasn't as big as possible."

"This is true," Holly agrees. "I can't even imagine what your bachelorette party will be like."

"Well, what's bigger than Vegas?" Pam asks wickedly.

"Yikes," Holly says. "I'm scared to find out."

"Holly, wouldn't you be the one to plan it?" I ask.

"No," she says. "Pam controls her own fate. I just go along for the ride."

We all laugh at this. I ask, "Will you have a long engagement, do you think?"

"Heck no," Pam says. "We're in love and can't wait to be married, living in the same house. We'd elope tomorrow if we could."

"Why can't you?" Holly asks. "He seems like a Vegas chapel, married-by-Elvis kind of dude."

"He does." *I agree with Holly.*

"No...I mean, I don't know. We obviously haven't had much discussion about it yet because we're in the finals at the moment. But I think my Georg is a beach-wedding-in-his-shorts kind of guy."

"Oh, I could see that, too!" Holly agrees emphatically.

I nod but the conversation ends as the opposing team scores. Everyone in the suite lets out a collective groan.

Pam swears and Holly frowns, pulling up her feeds.

As the clock winds down, Pam stands up and sighs loudly. "Off to the locker rooms," she says. "Scarlett, you coming back down to stare at the Mad Russian stud some more?"

Holly's neck looks like it might snap as she turns to look at me, a tiny quirk of her lips giving away her amusement. "Viktor?" she asks. "You were ogling Viktor?"

I shake my head. "No, I wasn't!"

"She totally was," Pam interjects. "But he was just as into her. Maybe this will be the next love connection at Crush Matchmaking HQ."

"No, I was just talking to him. He was upset that we were taking his picture."

Both women give me sly, knowing looks and I just

purse my lips and stand, ready to follow Pam out of the suite.

Holly yells, "Be careful of that one!"

Pam just cackles and I ignore them both as we make our way out to the elevator.

Totally busted.

We come into the hallway on the locker room level only to find a big throng of very loud, very hyped hockey players going in.

One of whom is in the process of removing his jersey. I know that big body. It's Viktor of course, but he doesn't make the turn in through the locker room door.

He just keeps coming right on down the tunnel. Jesus, he's even taller in skates...

And then he crashes straight into me.

4
"good-mood viktor"

Viktor

I must be getting older, because I cannot come off the ice without a chink or a cramp or some sort of pain in some part of my body. Today it's a muscle in my shoulder, so I pull off my jersey and pads as I walk down the tunnel, ready for the soothing hands of one of our therapy people.

Of course, walking and undressing is as ill-advised as it sounds, because I collide squarely into another human. I hear an *oof* sound, and as I pull the remainder of fabric over my head, I see Scarlett from earlier, on the ground glaring up at me.

"I am very sorry." Looking up, I see that I have walked several meters past the doorway to the locker room. "I must do better looking at where I am going."

I hold out a hand, which she takes, before standing and brushing off some imaginary dust or dirt from her jeans.

"Are you back for more photos?" She nods once,

briefly, and then bites her bottom lip again. *Maybe she is cringing? I hope I didn't hurt her.* "Are you all right?"

"I think so, yes. My booty to the rescue." She gives her ass a slap. "Plenty of padding to protect me."

I cannot help it; my eyes go straight to her ass. Yes, she is a curvy girl, but it is insanely attractive. "I would say the padding serves you well in several ways."

"So...the big guy likes a big butt?" She raises an eyebrow at me.

Totally caught off guard, I laugh out loud. I never laugh. Yet she made me laugh. Surprising. How she isn't angry or hurt is also a surprise. I'm not exactly small.

"Well, I appreciate yours—very much." I can feel the smile on my face as I look down at her and wonder whatever the fuck is wrong with me. I do not laugh or smile or flirt with women.

You're doing it with her right now, slaboumnyy. *If I am honest, I am behaving far worse than an imbecile at the moment.*

She tilts her head and twirls a piece of her long, red hair around her finger. "Well, that's nice to hear. And I appreciate a guy who knows when to take advantage of an opening."

I must look confused because she adds, "Nice shot out there. You scored."

I let out a breath and nod my head. "Yes, it was a surprise, but not unwelcome."

"No, I suppose scoring a goal in a championship game would be classified as welcome. Yep." She grins and winks. "I've got to go find Sid. Nice talking to you."

She starts to walk away, but I'm planted in place, watching that sexy ass of hers sway from side to side. I manage to bring a few of my brain cells back to full power and call out to her. "Hey Scarlett?"

She turns, her pretty face giving me a questioning look.

"Later you will have dinner with me?" In my head, I try to figure out if that came out right in English.

Her eyes go wide at this, and I cannot tell if I asked the wrong question, or the right one. But before she can answer, my agent, Vlad Nechaev, claps me on the back. I shake his hand as he congratulates me on my goal, but when I look back to get an answer from Scarlett, she's already gone. *Perhaps I did ask that wrong, after all.* Three years, and I still don't understand American women well. Oh well.

Vlad and I walk into the locker room and I climb onto an empty table as he tells me I need to set aside time to meet up with his associates in the next few days. I nod as Coach Brown kicks him out of the locker room with a terse, "No agents! Save it for after the game."

Vlad puts his hands up and gives an apologetic smile before slinking out into the hallway. Coach tells everyone to shut up and while the therapist works on my aching shoulder, we get notes on the second period.

"Congrats to Viktor, who recognized an opening and followed it to the net," Coach says. The guys cheer and I give a thumbs-up from my perch. The photographer, Sid, snaps another picture of me, and I glare at him. "Evan, they're all over you, but they can't be everywhere. Two of our three first-string defensemen have scored in this game. They won't know where to look, so keep lobbing shots on goal."

He goes on, telling us that at two-to-one, this game is nowhere near over, that he wants to see us finish strong, and then he promises a round of shots post-game if we win.

Kink worked out, I sit up and pull my pads and jersey hastily over my head, ready to head back out. Scarlett passes by and I reach out without thought to touch her wrist.

Her head nearly snaps turning to look at me.

"I am sorry to startle, but my offer of dinner stands."

"I'll think about it." She doesn't give me more than those few words, and I cannot read her. I have no idea if she is interested in having dinner with me. Usually, a woman's attention is easy to acquire. And it is safe to say that players in the NHL (or the KHL for that matter) do not have to work too hard to find females willing to spend time with them...generally, but with Scarlett, I'm truly unsure about her.

"I will be required for press." I scowl at the

thought because there is little I hate more than talking to the fucking press. "But will you find me after?"

Beautiful Red Rocket gives me a lopsided grin and another wink before walking away.

As we line up in the tunnel once more, Georg nudges a padded shoulder into me. "Scarlett, huh?" he asks conspiratorially.

"Red Rocket." I give a feral grin.

He nods in agreement. "She is that, yes. And a live wire, I hear. She and Pam are friends. She's got some baggage though."

"Doesn't matter," Tyler says from my other side. "He's just going to fuck her."

"Do not speak for me. I asked her to *dinner*—not to hook up."

"Don't be so uptight, big guy," Tyler says, bouncing from one skate to the other. "We all need to get our rocks off."

I roll my eyes and set my face to game mode, not giving the rookie the satisfaction of an answer. My interests, sexual or otherwise, are none of his fucking business. He broadcasts his exploits as if they are public information. I prefer my private life details to stay private.

"You'd think he'd be in a better mood after that goal," Tyler mutters.

"He is in a good mood," Georg says, snickering. "Can't you tell the difference between bad-mood Viktor and good-mood Viktor?"

There is positive energy as we take the ice again, the crowd loud as flashes from cameras and cell phones light up the arena. *Welcome to the Jungle* plays as we get in a quick warm-up skate before taking our positions. Tyler plays air guitar with his stick and Georg dances, as well. I like Guns N' Roses okay, I suppose. I prefer hardcore, Russian heavy metal. Bands like Arkona and Catharsis are more my style. Not that I will ever hear such bands play for American crowds of this size.

The period starts and I am in the game. Nothing else matters but winning this championship, and we all feel cocky as the action begins. Evan does as instructed, taking a shot on goal right off the bat, but never making it to the net. Mikhail takes a quick run as well, with me fighting to protect him, but his shot doesn't make it past the goalie.

A quick turnover and we get hung up trying to catch their best winger, who manages an impossible shot past our goalie, tying the game. Tyler's temper rages as he gets in the referee's face, calling for a penalty that did not occur, as far as I could see. Evan makes his way to play peacemaker, and we reset.

"This is it," Evan says to the defensive line. "Do not let another goal into that fucking net!"

I fucking won't.

5
really, really russian

Third period does not start well. I'm actually thankful to be focused on Sid's computer for a few minutes, missing the game-tying goal by the opposing team. I hear boos from the arena as we huddle over our photos, choosing images and writing captions that are more focused this time, less humorous. We send everything to Holly before I make my way back up to the suite.

I find Pam biting her nails by the window when I get there. We both watch the action on the ice in silence for a few moments. The brutal side of hockey is on full display as the two teams battle it out.

"It's getting really physical, and someone's going to get hurt." Pam voices exactly what I'm thinking.

I know she's worried about Georg. He's already had a bad concussion this season, among other injuries, that landed him in the hospital and on injured reserve for several weeks. "He'll be careful," I say quietly.

"Yeah," she says with a steadying exhale. "You're probably right. I just…"

"You worry. It's normal."

"It was really hard seeing my Georg like that. I don't think I've ever told anyone how scared I was. How it made me realize how much I cared for him."

"I know how that goes."

Pam puts her arm around my shoulder. "Yes, I'm sure you do. But maybe there's a bright spot emerging? With Viktor? I haven't seen his attention diverted by anyone before, so it was interesting watching him relate to you."

I shrug. To say I was surprised is an understatement. But the dinner invite? Never saw that coming. I thought those burly Russians didn't do dinner dates. *Pick and fuck.* That I'd heard many times before though. "He asked me to dinner tonight."

"Wow." Pam nudges my shoulder. "Are you going?"

"I don't know, I don't really know him…"

"No one really knows him."

"That's not helpful. He's so big and intimidating. And he's really, really Russian."

"So?" Pam laughs. "So's Georg."

"No," I say, shaking my head. "No. Georg is like one-tenth the level of Russian that Viktor is. Seriously. His accent is super thick. He looks like he could be a gangster. I swear he could snap someone's head off with the flick of a wrist. They call him the Mad Russian, for Christ's sake."

"Are you scared of him, Scarlett?"

"No. He's just...very imposing. He's intense. He complimented me and I felt like I needed a shower afterward. Not because it was icky, but because it got me all hot and bothered enough to start sweating. I felt like he shined a spotlight on me or something." Even though I've fantasized from afar for a while, I don't know if I can be around a guy who's so intense all the time. He's so...*fierce*.

"I'll bet the sex would be on the rough side with him."

"Right?" I agree. "Like, tie me up and spank my ass, big boy." I don't tell Pam that Viktor's compliment was about how much he appreciated my ass. Some things don't need to be shared. Plus, it would give her the wrong impression about him. He didn't say it in a creepy way. I was the one who brought up my plentiful posterior padding when he asked me if I was okay after falling on it. Viktor was very much a gentleman during our short conversation, so I cannot fault him there.

"Never know until you try," Pam says, grinning widely.

"Do you think he's in the mafia?"

"No, Scarlett. You asked the same thing about Georg once, remember?"

"But I'm serious this time. He has this creepy, Russian agent. He's like a snake, all slicked-back-hair and shiny suit. He even had a gold tooth."

"In the front?"

"No, on the side, but still…" I try to suppress a shudder as I remember him talking to Viktor in the hallway during the break. I didn't like the look of that guy. At all.

"Agents come in all shapes and sizes," Pam says dismissively. "Maybe looking slick is his normal style."

My scoff is interrupted by a conflict on the ice. Tyler, the middle defenseman, has gotten himself into yet another fight. It must not be too significant, though, because he only gets a two-minute penalty. There are three minutes left in the game.

Short-handed, the team works on killing the power play. They need to score, but on a five-four disadvantage, the best they can really hope for is to hold for a tie and then score in overtime.

The minutes seem to take forever, and at sixty seconds left on the clock, Tyler charges out of the box and back into position. Evan looks like he's got good control of the puck as he heads for the net. I think he might shoot the puck over to Mikhail or even back to Georg, but he doesn't, his focus laser-sharp on the goal.

He's so focused, in fact, that he doesn't seem to notice the defenseman coming from his left. Viktor does, though, and he charges. Way out of position, way fast, a freight train speeding off the track. He banishes the opposing defenseman to the glass in a blistering check that we can hear even here in the suite.

Of course, the penalty for charging is a major one, but a minor is called on the opposing team as well since the defenseman managed to high-stick Evan before Viktor checked him. Tyler is there again, trying to punch the guy Viktor just checked, and the referees are trying desperately to break up the melee. The buzzer goes off, ending third period with a tie, and forcing an overtime that will mean a four-three power play.

"This is just crazy," Pam says.

Holly has joined us at the windows. She links arms with Pam, a worried look on her face. Her husband, Evan, shakes off the fall, but with the cameras focused on his face, he looks pissed.

Viktor stomps into the box and sits heavily, staring blankly forward. The other player climbs into the opposing team's penalty box next to ours, with just a wall of glass separating the two spaces. Tyler follows, thumping down beside Viktor. The guy in the other box chirps something, but Viktor just shakes his head, giving away nothing. Tyler takes off his glove and gives the guy the middle finger before both teams must head off to the locker rooms for the next break.

The crowd is crazy rowdy—screaming, booing,

hissing. This is not a good end to a big game. We're not invited into the locker room for photos during the break. The players need to get their heads on straight before overtime begins and that means zero distractions from outside.

When the puck drops, Evan and Mikhail line up and poor Georg is left alone to play defense. The penalty clock starts a five-minute timer and the three best Crush players manage to hold off an onslaught of shots, doing their best for three full minutes before a specialty play creates confusion, allowing a shot that will, inevitably, give Washington, DC the Stanley Cup.

It's a huge let down and ending to such an intense game along with a very hard-fought season.

The teams line up for the handshake, but I can see on their faces how upset they all are. I can feel it in the suite here, too. Holly goes straight into work mode, her dedication to her work belying her emotion on behalf of her husband and the team she loves so much.

Fiona pulls me over and we talk about how we'll communicate the loss, what language we'll use, and what imagery we'll promote post-game. Holly has the immediate work to do, but I'll have to craft a press packet and pitch a series of positive story ideas tomorrow. We come up with our plan and then head down to the press room to set up for the post-game conference.

There are screens set up in the room, post-game

on as our crew makes sure the microphones are ready and chairs are in the right spots. The cup is awarded to the other team on *our* ice. Fiona scowls at the imagery it creates on television. Holly just types away on her iPad.

Members of the press start to arrive shortly after, including Kacey King, the blonde, too-skinny reporter who, I've heard, likes to screw the players. I think she's done it with both Evan and Georg, so Pam and Holly have equal distaste for her. Today she's in an emerald-green miniskirt, black blouse, and tall, black heels. I'll give it to her; she knows how to look sexy for the camera.

My news alerts start going off. Social media feeds are obviously the first to ping, since Holly is putting out congratulatory messages on all our feeds, as well as retrospective images that remind our fans how good our season was.

Evan, Georg, and Viktor come in, hair wet from the showers, and sit at the table. Reporters call out questions, and while they focus mostly on the loss, there are bright spots as they get to talk about the way the defense scored both of this game's goals. Evan, always the leader, remains focused on the positive. Georg makes a few jokes to cool things down. Viktor only answers those questions he has to. That isn't a surprise, of course. The man is...reticent.

I find myself staring at him. He is a very handsome man. I guess that goes without saying.

He's got tan skin and dark brown hair in an undercut, the sides and back shaved short but the top longer. His gaze is super intense—although, what color eyes does he have? I should have taken more note earlier when he spoke to me. His lips are on the full side. Not too full, but definitely sensual. I could look at him for a loooong time. Yep, definitely easy on my eyes.

Lost in my inspection of the sexy Russian enforcer, I don't realize the press conference has ended until he rises from his chair, that intense stare leveled on me. He steps from behind the table and takes a few long strides in my direction.

I raise a hand in an awkward wave, ready to accept his offer of dinner, but he breezes right past me. He doesn't even acknowledge me. No, he just walks right on by like I don't exist, heads out through the door and down the hall.

Well shine me on why don't you.

Pam wanders up next to me and says, "Weren't you supposed to…"

"I thought so…but I guess I was wrong."

"Oh. Well, that's lame."

"Yup." Lame is exactly whatever that just was.

"Do you want to go to dinner with me and Georg?"

"Ah, I don't want to be a third wheel. You two just got engaged. I'm sure you should be off having hot sex in a bathtub full of chocolate or something."

She barks a laugh at this. "I wasn't aware that chocolate-covered bathtub sex was part of engagement celebrations."

"Chocolate-covered bathtub sex?" Georg asks as he comes over, pulling Pam in for a hot kiss. When he pulls away, he's grinning. "That sounds really sticky... and fun."

"Anything edible sounds tasty right now," Pam says. "And Viktor seems to have stood up Scarlett at the last minute, so we should go fill our bellies and eat our emotions together. I'm famished."

"Me too," Georg says. "Come on, Scarlett."

I agree, albeit somewhat reluctantly. I really do feel like a third wheel, but it beats going home to wonder what I did to turn Viktor away so quickly.

We walk a few blocks to a small restaurant that's kind of off the beaten path. It's definitely not a tourist destination because the locals welcome Georg as we walk in. We're seated at a semi-private table and champagne is brought out to celebrate Pam and Georg's engagement.

We make small talk for a while, then get more serious as we talk about the game. Georg tries to brush it off, but I can tell he's upset about the loss. He and Pam hold hands across the table most of the time leading up to our food being served. It's really cute and, once again, makes me long to have someone who loves me that much.

Pam must sense my emotions because she tilts

her head and asks me to tell her about my ex-boyfriend.

"Stephen." I take in a big breath. Let it out. Take in another one. Just saying his name gives me anxiety. "I met him in high school. He left to go to college but moved back a year later. He'd been playing cards on the East Coast. Started out innocent enough. He was into role-playing games and stuff as a teenager, but I guess he started playing the real card games in college. Also betting on sports and fantasy leagues. And he was good at it, too. He banked a bunch of money and decided to quit college and come back to Vegas. He got into some lower-level poker tournaments but quickly rose to the higher-stakes games. He had backers, funders, and played in the world series games with celebrities."

"Stephen Hackworth?" Georg asks.

"You knew him?"

He shakes his head, his face serious. "No. I heard of him, though. People talked about how young he was to be so good. He died, right?"

"Georg!" Pam scolds.

"It's okay. He did die." The next part hurts me to say the words out loud. "He committed suicide. At least, that's what the police say."

"You don't agree?" Georg asks.

"I don't know, honestly."

The waitress brings our entrees. Suddenly, my stomach is sour. I doubt I'll be able to eat this big bowl of pasta I ordered.

"Stephen started using a lot, stuff to keep him awake for these all-night games. And he started losing. He lost sports bets and then he lost poker games. And then he was in debt. Lots of it. We'd gotten engaged the year before. I was barely twenty and I liked the celebrity of it all, being on his arm. And he didn't seem to worry too much at all the losses. Not at first. He seemed really calm about it, saying things like, 'everything ebbs and flows, babe.'"

"When did you start to worry?" Pam asks.

"When two huge, scary Russians came to the door and roughed me up. Said he owed a ton of money to their boss. Threatened to come back and do worse if he didn't materialize soon with their cash."

"Oh my God, Scarlett. No wonder you're paranoid about the Russian mob!" Pam reaches out and takes my hand across the table. "How terrifying for you."

"He came home and found me in a corner, bloody and shaking. We had a huge argument and he told me not to worry. He said he had a big tournament to play and he was going to get everything he owed them and more. Then he would quit, and we'd get married and go live somewhere else. He said he'd get a regular job, go back to school. But he lost the tournament and the goons came back and I ended up in the hospital with two fractured ribs. And while I was in there, the police came and told me Stephen had killed himself. Took a whole bottle of painkillers and chased it with a side of methamphetamine."

"Oh, fuck." Georg leans back in his chair with wide eyes.

"Pretty much that, yeah." I nod my head slowly. I can still see every moment of that night. I was in so much pain and had been feeling so lonely, angry why Stephen hadn't come to the hospital to see me. The look on the policeman's face as he'd told me my fiancé was dead...had killed himself. The pity. I remember turning away from their pitiful expressions in a state of shock. Pain. Grief. Anger. *Why had he taken the coward's way out?* I was too terrified to ask if it meant the Russians would still be coming after me...*what would they do if they did come? Would I ever be safe?* I can feel the same tremors of fury and sadness starting.

Pam leans across the table and holds my hand, a very cold hand from such a painful recall.

"I'm so sorry, Scarlett." Pam's expression is grim. "You were twenty years old?"

"Yep. It was almost two years ago. That year pretty much sucked."

"I don't know what to say, honey," Pam says gently.

"Dammit." I wipe away a tear that has managed to roll down my cheek. "I'm just a mess. I'm so sorry. This is such a downer on a night that should be all about celebrating the two of you."

"It's okay," Pam says with a squeeze to my hand.

"Yeah, it's okay. We are glad we could accompany you tonight. And I will also happily kick Viktor in the balls for standing you up." Georg's accent and more formal speech comes out a little louder than usual. I've noticed he does that whenever the topic veers to serious. He's not always the comedian.

I laugh at his threat of violence to Viktor's cojones. "No need. I wasn't sure I wanted to go out with him anyway."

"He is a bit of a stick in the mud," Georg offers. "For real. His mood is very serious. No fun at all."

"Now, now," Pam says, shaking her head. "He can be kind and polite too, Georg. Give him some credit for being a mostly decent guy. We can't all have your charming personality, now can we?"

Georg shuts her up with a kiss across the table.

We finish dinner on lighter topics, and I find myself emotional as I take a cab home. I wait until I get inside my small apartment, but then lose it as soon as the door is locked behind me. I head straight into the shower and weep as the hot water rains down on my body, cleaning away the pain of the past. Or, at least, I wish it would. I still have so many things hanging over my head. Not just Stephen's death, but his remaining debt. And my father...

It's all too much sometimes. So, it's probably best that I didn't go out with a possibly shady Russian hockey player tonight anyway. Who needs that drama? *Not. Me.*

Even though said Russian hockey player is incredibly hot.

Insanely hot.

And pushes every single one of my buttons.

But, thanks to Viktor's rebuttal tonight, I'll never know what it would feel like for him to push any buttons. My life doesn't need another complication. It's time to close off that one-sided, poorly timed attraction and stay focused on moving forward.

Hot hockey players be damned.

6
not fun for parties

Viktor

I soak in the ice bath beneath the arena for a long time. Long enough that it burns, thinking and rethinking my stupidity in charging that player.

Sometimes I am too aggressive on the ice. This was one of those times, and it cost us the championship. I have only myself to blame.

Therapy staff mill around, assisting with minor injuries. One of them tells me I'll do myself damage if I don't get out of the tub, so I rise, the cold water sluicing over my skin. I grab a robe and head for the sauna, wanting the extreme difference of cold and hot to calm my aching muscles.

Nothing can calm my mind, though.

I did the wrong thing. Tyler did the wrong thing. But I also protected our captain from what was bound to be an injury-causing check against the boards. I should not have earned a major penalty though. A five-minute penalty? Really?

"Fuck!" Punching the wall of the sauna does nothing but bruise my knuckles and put a dent in the wood.

I remember looking up at the owner's suite from the penalty box. I expected everyone to be staring at me. To be just as angry with me as I was with myself. I saw so many familiar faces up there, watching through the row of glass windows. Evan's wife, Holly. Georg's fiancée, Pamela. And yes, the beautiful Scarlett as well. And they were watching with worry, their faces full of concern and caring. But not anger.

With the game lost, it turned my stomach to shake their hands, to see the other team skate the cup across our ice. And I do think of this as *our ice*. Crush ice. My home now. My team. And I have sorely let them down.

A call to my cell phone in the locker room reminds me that I have to meet Vlad and his associates tomorrow. There is a big MMA fight and he's got ringside seats set up for us. I'd hoped it would be a celebratory outing, that I'd be high on the championship. Now, I'm angry enough that I'd very much like to get into that ring myself.

I went up to the press conference like a dutiful dog, but I said as little as possible. Georg and Pamela's engagement was still big news, and the questions that came my way were about my goal, not my fuckup, so that was a relief. However, I could not focus my own energy on the positive. No, all I felt was loss. Like a loser. And when I saw Scarlett, her hand raised in greeting, I simply could not face her. There was no way she'd want to go out with the defense loser. She never even said yes, so surely she wasn't expecting me to stop to talk to her.

I head home exhausted. Miserable. I do end up going to the MMA fight, but I can barely muster the energy to care much about it. I get as drunk as I can, my mood souring with each beer I drink. Vlad tells me to cool it, but I don't. In fact, I drink more just to spite him because he is annoying when he tells me what to do. He is not my father. He works for me. He is paid to do the job of representing me, nothing more.

The next morning, I've got a text from Georg and a pounding headache. He calls me an enormous prick for standing up Scarlett. I don't respond out of guilt. Georg is correct. I was a prick for doing that to her after I *twice* asked her to have dinner with me. He texts again a few minutes later.

Georg: I will probably regret this, but we're having our engagement party tomorrow night.

Georg: You should come.

Viktor: I am not fun for parties.

Georg: You are not fun for anything. But you should still come. Asshole.

Viktor: Where?

Georg: LINQ hotel. 7 p.m.

Viktor: Ok

Georg: See you at closing meeting today.

I don't answer. I forgot about closing meeting. This is a chance to get final thoughts from Coach Brown, clean out our lockers, and do any last press.

While I would rather stay inside the dark cave of my apartment, I drag myself out of bed, hung over as I may be, and run a hot shower. I drink leftover, cold coffee straight from the pot, and then head out.

At close-out, Coach basically threatens me and Tyler. If we do not get it together and stop causing unnecessary fights and penalties, he will send us back to the minors. Not that I ever played in any minor league here in the United States. I played professional hockey for the Russian national team since I was seventeen. I also played in two Olympics before I joined an East Coast NHL team for two years. And now one year here in Vegas.

I know what he is saying, though. He took our trade. He wanted a championship-winning defensive line. And there is potential here. We all know it. But we also blew it. The minors, for me, might mean just sitting on a bench while he gives someone else a shot on first-string. I did not come to the US to sit on a bench.

We clean out our lockers and then the press is allowed in to get individual thoughts on the series and the season. I barely get approached, probably because I am an asshole. But the blonde reporter named Kacey King does come over to talk to me. She gushes over my goal, her hand on my arm while we talk. When the camera goes off, she asks the cameraman to meet her at the van. He just shrugs and stalks off.

I assume we're done but she follows me as I make my way to the door. She touches my arm again and asks me if I have any plans for the evening. She wears a very revealing dress, too revealing for any self-respecting reporter. But I know this woman's reputation. And I know what she is asking me. And for a moment, I consider it.

She is very small, very thin. Attractive, but in a way that seems fake. And there is desperation there, too. It is not an uncommon thing, seeing a woman hide her desperation under fake sexual bravado. The puck bunnies who try to get with players are commonly like this, which is why they so turn me off. I want a real woman, a woman who is not masking insecurity by screwing someone famous.

But there is a small part of me that considers Kacey. Perhaps bending her over the back of my couch and plowing into her would calm my heavy sense of disappointment for a little while. Perhaps a moment of pleasure, of release, would be beneficial to me right now.

"I do," I finally say. "I am expected elsewhere, unfortunately."

"Oh," she says, forcing a smile. "Okay. I'll hope for a rain check, then. It would be fun to get to know you better. It's been a pleasure watching you play this season."

She struts off, flicking her long hair back as her high heels click against the floor.

My hand will have to do for tonight.

Once again.

7

the bosses do not have to know

Scarlett

I work up a post-game press release that celebrates the team's great season. Holly has put out a series of congratulatory social media posts to go along with the many quotes and notable moments I included in my release. I've got three story ideas to pitch, as well, so I work those up and send them to Fiona to review before I email them to our contacts.

Fiona is down in the locker rooms making sure the players all stick to a prescribed plan for how we will downplay our loss and focus on our team's positive efforts. It's all highly orchestrated, but whatever. She's a master at all of this. I just do as I'm told.

Once I'm done for the day, I head out to shop for a dress to wear to Georg and Pam's impromptu engagement party. They plan to get married really quickly, and though they're still working out the plans, they want to get everyone together to follow up the loss with something positive. I decide that, fraternization policy or not, I am going to flirt up one of the Crush players there and see where it leads. I deserve a little fun for once. It's a party and it's a hotel, and I'm pissed that Viktor stood me up. And I'm extra pissed that I allowed myself to dwell on Stephen and his bullshit for so long last night. My eyes are still puffy from crying. Freaking irritating.

I have to work my second job tonight and I don't have much time, so speed-shopping it is. I search the sale racks until I find what I think is a knockout. It's green and strapless and short. I'm elated when I find a pair of strappy silver sandals to go with the green and call it a day.

Of course, my uniform of a metallic gold-fringed corset paired with black butt shorts is standard slutty issue for my job as a cocktail waitress at the Tangiers. It's mindless work, taking drink orders, answering stupid gambling questions, ignoring leering men, shoving the occasional wandering hand away from my ass. My coworkers tease me that I'd get better tips if I smiled and allowed the wandering hands a bit more.

Nah. I am not that dedicated to a job I wish like hell I didn't have to work. *Thank you, Stephen, for fucking up my life even when you're dead.* Would I only ever know assholes?

As usual, I'm an angry, pissed-off cocktail waitress as I make my way home. The only bonus comes with the sleep in until noon the next day. It's rare that I get to do that, and I relish the feeling of my soft bed and pillows until I get a series of texts from Pam.

> Pam: Come over early. Have a hairstylist on hand.

> Pam: We can drink and get ready together.

> Pam: You can see the amazing suite Georg got for us for the week.

> Pam: Are you even awake?

> Pam: Get your ass up and over here, girl.

> Scarlett: Okay, okay

> Scarlett: I'm up. I'll be over in a bit.

> Pam: There's mimosas and food and chocolate.

> Scarlett: On my way. You said chocolate.

I shower and leave my hair wet as I pull on some shorts and a T-shirt, my things for the day and tonight packed in a bag. The party will be on a private deck with a private pool and bar, but Pam is holed up in a vast suite with bright, white furniture and a view of sprawling Las Vegas.

She's not wrong. There is a ton of food— croissants, fruit, bacon, eggs—and mimosas. Rich-smelling coffee, and an array of specialty desserts as well.

"Why so much food?" I ask as I wander around the suite, taking in the views internal and external.

"The chocolates were a gift from Max Terry. The brunch stuff was just for fun."

"Cool." I load up a plate and doctor a cup of coffee with sugar and milk.

"Holly's on her way. She's currently micromanaging her uncle Troy, who is staying with the baby until tomorrow at noon," Pam says. She snickers at the thought. "Poor Uncle Troy."

"Why?" I ask with a mouth stuffed with flaky pastry goodness. "Dany seems like a really good baby."

"No, the baby's fine. Holly's a little overprotective."

"Oh. She probably parents the same way she works. With gusto."

We both giggle at this. We've come a long way, to be able to joke about Pam's best friend like this. Pam used to get defensive if I said anything at all about Holly. But it was just my insecurity showing with the job at the time, and honestly, Holly is amazing. I've grown to really like her as a coworker and as a friend. She's even a bit of a career mentor, to be honest. But she is also a person who takes her work and her family super seriously. And I doubt she's been away from her baby for this long since she was born.

Soon, the team nutritionist, Devon, arrives, and

Holly comes maybe an hour later. It's obvious she's been crying, even though she tries to cover it by giving us all a big smile.

"That bad?" Pam asks.

Holly's smile turns to a grimace and she flops onto the overstuffed couch. "I'm such a mess," she admits. "Troy was happy to stay with her but I just couldn't leave. Dany didn't even notice I was leaving. Evan was ready to go. It was just me being a blubbering mess. And I know it's only, like, twenty-four hours, but…"

"It's your first time away," Pam says, pulling her into a side-hug. "It'll get easier, Holls."

"What are the guys doing today?" I ask, trying to get her thinking about something other than the baby.

"Evan got us a suite for the night, too. They're drinking and doing whatever dudes do," Holly says. "Hopefully, it doesn't look and smell like some bachelor pad by the time we get to enjoy it tonight."

"Hopefully, you'll be able to relax long enough to enjoy it tonight," Pam comments.

"Ten bucks says they'll be home by midnight," Devon says, grinning from the food table.

"I'll take that bet," I say. "I have faith in you, Holly."

"Well, thank you, Scarlett," Holly says. She takes a steadying breath. "Tonight's going to be fun. I am actually really excited about getting dressed up and having a night in a hotel with my hot husband."

"I'd be excited, too," I say.

"Maybe you and Viktor could—" Pam starts.

"No," I say, putting a hand up to stop her. "No. Viktor and I cannot anything. We are *not* a thing. We're not even friends."

"He seems intense," Devon comments.

"Exactly," I say. "And he asked me out then ignored me, so..."

There's a knock on the door so I use it as an opportunity to escape any more conversation about Viktor Demoskev. It's Daisy, another of our media department coworkers. She's a pretty girl, kind of quiet and low-key. She sits in the cubicle across from Holly and manages media credential requests. I didn't realize she even knew Pam.

She comes in and looks around, obviously uncomfortable. She's one of those women who still looks like a girl. She's probably older than she looks but she wears little makeup and usually has her long dark hair pulled back in a ponytail. She had a long-term boyfriend but broke up with him recently. She doesn't say much, so I don't know why, but I do know he made a really big scene for her at work. I thought she might conjure a hole to bury herself in, honestly. She's pretty shy. Yet, she's here today and I was glad. I wasn't the only single girl, so there was comfort in that.

We finish eating and decide to go to the pool for a swim and some sun before showering and getting ready for the party. Of course, the guys are all there when we arrive. And Viktor is among them. My heart kind of leaps when I see him, but then I remember how pissed I am at him. He looks good though. Pretty impossible for him not to look good in nothing but a pair of board shorts and all those tan muscles on full display.

He saunters up, lips set in that hot perma-scowl of his.

"Hello, Red Rocket." His thick accent rolling off his tongue like sex dipped in chocolate with not a single care in the world.

"Red Rocket?" What the hell? But then I get it. I've heard some of the guys call women "rockets" before. And I have red hair, so... "That's kind of gross, you know." I cringe. "Dogs get red rockets when they're sexually excited. I don't think I like that name."

"I assure you it is a term of endearment," he says softly, his eyes on my lips. "And with dogs, it means they like you."

"Ah...Viktor? You're not helping your case, not even a little bit. No." I shake my head at him. "And thanks for standing me up after the game, by the way."

"It was not a good night. I was not fit to be good company for you."

"Well, a hello and a request for a rain check would have been nice," I snap.

He shrugs, seemingly unapologetic. "We will try again another time."

"No, we won't. I don't get burned twice."

"It was not a burn. It was a hard loss that I did not take well, but it was not my intention to offend."

"Whatever." I raise my hands in mock surrender. "It's probably for the best. We have a no-fraternization policy and I doubt the bosses would let another one slide."

He steps closer, looming over me as he lowers his voice to a sexy rumble. "The bosses do not have to know."

Something about his voice. The deepness of it. The accent. The commanding tone. Whatever it is sends crazy electron insanity to my lady parts. I can't let him see that, though. He doesn't get off that easy.

Though "getting off" might be a fun way to spend this party...

No. NO, Scarlett. There are other hot guys out there. You can—and should—go find one of them and stay away from this possible mafia goon who never smiles.

I step away from him and put my hand on his bicep. It's big. Like really big. This guy is insanely ripped.

What was I going to say, again?

Oh, yeah... "Thanks, but no thanks. Have fun at the party."

I manage to tear my hand away from his bicep (even though I was really into feeling it) and saunter toward the bar. I get a beer and then find a soft lounge chair to sink into under an umbrella. Daisy, awkward as ever, sits next to me.

"I'm surprised to see you here, Daisy."

"Oh, I just...Holly asked me to come," she says, nursing some kind of pink, frothy, girly drink that has a tiny umbrella in it.

"Well, who knows? Maybe you'll hook up with one of these hot hockey studs."

She shakes her head. "No, big sports guys aren't my type."

"Oh yeah? What kind of guys are your type?"

"Oh, I don't know. I like guys who like to camp and read and hike."

"Hipsters, then?" I ask, grinning.

She giggles. "Maybe? What about you? What's your type?"

This is the most I've ever heard Daisy talk. She talks to Holly, but anyone can talk to Holly. I mull the question. "Hmm. Not sure. I don't think I have a type, per se, but I do know I attract assholes."

She cringes. "Really?"

I nod, pouting for dramatic effect. "My first boyfriend in high school got my best friend pregnant."

"Oh, no!"

"Right? My second boyfriend told me to lose an, *acceptable to him*, amount of weight or he wouldn't take me to prom that year. He would let me know when I was presentably skinny enough to be his date."

"Yikes," Daisy says, wincing. "Did you?"

"I did not," I answer proudly. "I told him exactly

where to shovel his bullshit two seconds after the words came out of his idiot mouth. Those extra two seconds were needed for me to gather my opinion of his absurd proposition."

Daisy laughs and nods her head. "Oh good."

"Then my fiancé...he was a wreck. Big gambling addiction, drugs...he committed suicide." She starts to open her mouth and I shake my head. "Don't. People always say they're sorry, but it's fine. I'm over it."

"Are you dating anyone now?"

"Nah. I flirt around but I just really want to find someone good, you know? Someone who will treat me right. I'm ready for love but I'm not going to allow myself to fall for someone shady again. No way."

"Does Viktor Demoskev count as shady?" she asks timidly. "I saw him flirting with you over there."

"Ugh," I groan. "Yes, he does. Definitely something shady going on there."

Some of the players wind up over by us and we make small talk with them about their plans for the summer. I didn't realize it, but many of them apparently go overseas and play summer leagues, often for their home countries. This allows them to stay connected to opportunities to represent their countries in some capacity when the Winter Olympics roll around every four years.

It's a fun group including some of Pam's friends from grad school who have come in for the party as well. We all play in and around the pool until late-afternoon, when the wedding planner kicks us all out so she can direct setup for the evening's festivities.

Pam and the wedding planner converse as the crowd heads back in and up to various suites and hotel rooms. Daisy and I make our way back up to the suite, finding Holly already in the room, in tears.

"What's wrong?" I ask. "I didn't even see you down at the pool this afternoon."

She tries to give me a smile, as if I'm the one who needs reassurance. I sit next to her and she sniffles as she says, "I don't know. I'm just feeling really emotional right now."

"Maybe you're PMSing?"

She lifts a shoulder. "I need to get it together. I'm supposed to be here for my best friend and I'm on the couch crying like a baby. And was Evan down there?"

I nod. "I saw him once or twice. Just talking to some of the guys."

She gives a sad, resigned face. "Good. I'm glad I didn't ruin his afternoon."

She doesn't say any more, and I don't want to ask. I like Holly a lot, but I don't know her well enough to be in her marital or parenting drama. I mean, she and Evan are like a totally dream couple. They're gorgeous and perfect and successful. What could possibly be wrong in their little world?

I decide to jump in the shower before anyone else claims it, and I spend the whole time feeling resentful. Toward Holly, for crying like that when she has a perfect life. A perfect husband. A perfect baby.

A perfect career. I lost my fiancé to gambling and drugs. And my father is totally MIA. I should be the one crying, not her.

When I come out of the bathroom, the hairdresser and makeup person have arrived. Pam is still talking to the wedding planner, and Holly has now joined them. She's put on a brave face, stopped crying, and actually looks pretty and happy for the moment. I hear her ask, "This week, really?"

I wander over to the hair station and the woman's eyebrows raise as I sit. She leans in and says, "Hunker down, sister. Looks like you'll be living at the LINQ this week."

"Why?" I ask, confused. "What did I miss?"

"Looks like Pam and Georg have decided to tie the knot at the end of this week! They're moving up to the wedding suite and they've asked everyone to hang out all week to party and celebrate up to the big event."

"Whoa," I say. "Wow. They literally just got engaged."

She grins as she combs out my long, wet, tangled hair. "They're eager to get their lives started, I guess."

Pam confirms a little bit later, as the stylist puts my crazy hair into an elaborate, braided up-do. "You look so good," she says. "Did you hear the news?"

"I did," I say, making a face I hope is a happy one. "This week, huh?"

She jumps up and down, clapping her hands.

"The hotel is totally up for helping us make it happen. All of our friends are here. Why not?"

"Well, I can't..." I start to speak but then feel ashamed. My cheeks flush. I push my lips together and breathe in and out through my nose.

"You can't afford to stay here for a few more days?" Pam asks quietly.

"You got it."

"It's okay," she says. "I mean, we're moving to the penthouse and this suite's already paid for. Why don't you stay in this one?"

"Oh, I couldn't...that's too much," I stammer. "Plus, I've got my other job to get to."

"And it's probably closer to here than your apartment, right? I insist. It's paid for already. Just use it, Scarlett."

"Are you sure?"

"Of course! That way you can let loose and be close to all the events. We'll do the engagement party tonight, of course, then the rehearsal dinner on Thursday and the wedding on Friday. And you can stay in the suite until Saturday noon."

"I guess that's a yes then." She is making some very good points. Not only that, I *need* this. I've never had luxury, never expected it either. But if my friend wants me to spend a few days in the lap of luxury, celebrating her love? That I can do. Although, that does mean buying another dress or possibly two.

"Yay," Pam cheers, jumping up and down. "Your hair looks amazing, by the way."

"She's got good hair," the stylist comments. She looks at her watch before telling Pam to move her butt and get in the shower.

Hair complete, I move to the makeup chair, and then finally manage to get into my dress and heels. I feel really good. Sexy. My dress fits like a glove, even though I got it on the sale rack. Devon whistles at me from her perch on the couch.

Of course, she's ridiculously beautiful with no makeup on. I swear she's like a Barbie clone or something. I can't believe she's a nutritionist counselor for a hockey team and not a supermodel. I don't know her very well. She's become friends with Pam, though I heard that Devon and Georg were very close "friends." So who knows what the story is there. Devon seems cool now and really happy for Pam and Georg.

I realize, as everyone gets dressed and ready, that I feel like an outsider. I mean, Pam and I have definitely hung out before. But Holly is her best friend, and she and Devon seem close. Daisy seems totally in her own world. And then there's me. I'm social. Sociable. I try to make knowing the office gossip my business, so I know people's names and faces and stories.

But I feel alone.

I know what it really is.

I'm lonely.

It's not a new feeling either, but is it actually one that can be fixed?

8
did you just smell me?

Scarlett

've put on my "flirt face." That's what my dad used to call it—the face I make when I'm trying to act like I don't have a care in the world. I try to wear that face at work, because I know I can get bigger tips when I look like I'm even remotely interested in the overweight rich guy who starts playing on tilt and ordering shots for the table. It's all a big fat lie because I happen to know from experience those kinds of guys usually tip for shit.

I think I've had, ohhhh, three beers now? And a tiny plate of delicious appetizers with names I can't pronounce. Probably need to increase my food-to-alcohol ratio at some point here.

Pam looks amazing. She's got her blonde hair styled in beachy waves. Her makeup is fierce, a dark liner and smoky shadow on her eyelids. She's in a sleek, short, black dress and I've caught Georg sneaking his hand up her crotch several times through the night. He can't keep his hands off her, actually. It's sweet to see people so in love that they can't control themselves in public.

"Those two are gonna fuuuuuuccckkkk tonight," Tyler sings beside me at the bar. He's obviously seen the same little things I've seen tonight.

"Indeed," I agree with a slow nod. "I mean, she's lookin' hot."

"She is, but so are you, lady."

"Well, thank you, sir." I take in Tyler, all broad-shouldered, All-American boy. He can't be much more than twenty-three. He made his debut in the NHL just last year mid-season.

"I see why he likes you," Tyler comments.

"Who?"

"Viktor. Duh."

"Viktor doesn't like anyone." I sniff. "Plus, he blew it anyway. He stood me up on game night."

"Well, to be fair, his dumb-ass penalty cost us the game. He would've been shitty company anyway."

I laugh. "Didn't you also have a dumb-ass penalty as well?"

He just sticks out his tongue. "I did a normal level of dumb-assery. He did an extra level."

"Okay, whatever you have to tell yourself so you can sleep at night."

Suddenly, I feel him at my back. Looming. My cheeks heat as Tyler says, "Hey, big guy. Just keepin' your seat warm for ya."

Tyler winks and hops off the bar stool so Viktor

can take his place. How did I know he was there before a single word was said? Am I that in tune to his body already? No. I can't be. It's just that he's so big. He takes up space.

And right now, he's taking up all the space right next to me.

Viktor

"YOU LOOK...GOOD," I say, taking in the luscious sight of her. Her legs look a mile long, pale in the evening light. Her skin is creamy. Especially the swell of her breasts against the green of her dress. I would love to help her out of that little dress. I imagine what is underneath must be spectacular.

"Mmm," she grunts, clearly unimpressed with the compliment. "Thanks."

I lean in, closer, and closer still until my lips nearly touch the exposed skin of her long neck. I inhale. She smells fresh, clean, slightly floral. My cock twitches as I imagine if her pussy tastes the same.

"You smell good enough to eat." My breath hits her skin, raising telltale goose bumps.

She uncrosses and re-crosses her legs. Was that a little squeeze I just detected? Is she as affected by me as I am by her?

"You're being creepy." She turns away from me

and takes a sip of her beer. "You can't just go around smelling people."

I chuckle darkly, without humor. "I think you're just saying that because you liked it. And I think you would like other things I could do to you."

"Well, you won't be doing a single thing, because I still haven't forgiven you for crapping out on me after the game."

She sits primly, her back ramrod straight, her legs tightly crossed. Even her rosebud mouth is pursed. I'd like to kiss it into submission. I'd like to make her come until she's boneless, relaxed, high on pleasure. Since when have I been so fixated on a woman? Or on her pleasure? It has been a very long time.

"But I have not asked for your forgiveness."

"You're smug for a guy who's trying to get into my panties."

I sigh heavily. I like this woman. She is feisty and beautiful. I want her badly. But I need her to understand that it was not a rejection of *her*. "Perhaps it will make you feel better to know I drank myself into oblivion that night. And the next, for that matter. I do not like to lose. I would have been very poor company for you."

"Georg said that. The last part, about being bad company. Though he also said you're a stick in the mud and no fun even on a good day," she babbles. I think she is maybe a little bit drunk.

"He is not wrong."

"You know, that glowing self-endorsement really makes me want to jump in the sack with you."

"Sexual gratification does not require fun, Scarlett. It only requires skill, practice, and concentration."

"Like hockey?" She gives me a little smirk that makes my dick hard.

"Yes, like hockey."

"Hmmm...still not selling me. Better go try that act on someone else."

"No." I lean in close again. I see the hunger in her eyes when she meets my gaze, the dark desire of attraction. She feels every bit of this attraction same as me. "I said I do not like to lose. It is now my mission to win you, Scarlett. At least for the night."

Scarlett

I GASP A LITTLE. This guy is a caveman, but something about him is totally revving me up. The way he smelled me; I knew he was thinking about other parts of my body. It made my nipples hard and I was thankful for the strong lining in this dress, or I'd have been putting out signals loud and clear as to just how affected my body was by his naughty act.

He gives just a shadow of a grin. Just one edge of one side of his totally kissable mouth lifts nearly imperceptibly. Damn. He heard that little noise. I look away and attempt to gather my wits again.

"I don't want to be won for a night." I take a sip of my drink. "I'm not a prize. I am not a commodity. This isn't a game. And I'm also not some gross jersey chaser that stands in line hoping to be chosen for a quick bang in the janitor's closet."

"People do this in the janitor's closet?"

I roll my eyes. "I don't know. I wasn't being literal about the location. You're missing my point."

"No, I am not," he insists. "I know that you are saying you are not interested in a one-night stand. This I understand."

"Then can you understand that I want something real? That I want a real connection? And the fact that you're a big celebrity athlete won't change that for me. There are probably twenty women at this party alone who would gladly go screw the famous Mad Russian in your hotel room. I am not one of them."

"I am sorry...my English is—" He rubs a thumb over his bottom lip in a move that should be illegal before asking, "Were you being literal about the location that time?"

I honestly can't tell if he's just messing with me, or if he's serious. I just raise an eyebrow in response. "Why am I even still talking to you? You're just another horny player trying to score for the night. And it's not going to be me!"

I'm about to say more, but I see Fiona and realize I still represent the team, especially in a setting like this. I don't want to make a scene, and I don't want her getting on my case for socializing with a player.

Though…what a joke that fraternizing policy is. First Evan and Holly got past it, then Pam and Georg. And I hear that Pam and Georg got caught on camera, screwing in the therapy room. So, if she still has a job after that, then…

I let out a little *pffft* sound just thinking about it. Viktor looks perplexed, surely wondering where my mind went just now. I just shake my head and hop off my stool. Straightening my dress and grabbing my clutch, I head out of the pool and party area.

I can feel the heat of Viktor's eyes on me every step of the way.

My feet take me to the elevator and down a few levels to a smaller, quieter bar. I take a seat at the counter and order myself another beer. I just need to think, to be away from the work stuff and from hulking, hot Viktor. I think I've handled him pretty well, considering. But still, he's terribly distracting. And we all know how easily I can be distracted by some hard muscles and a good set of lips. I remind myself that I don't need what he's offering. I don't need quick and easy.

Even if the quick and easy he's suggesting is hot enough to melt me from the inside out.

9
apologies

Viktor

I nurse my drink for a moment, feeling like an asshole. I don't flirt with women often. In fact, it's been a long time since. In the past few years, sex has been an indulgence for me, easily attained with minimal effort. Really only maintenance when I was in a mood. The last time was when I first came to the Crush with Tyler Lockhardt and we went out to a bar with Georg and some others after our first win on our new team. At least six months ago.

When I was sixteen, my coach told me that true athletes could not maintain long-term romantic relationships. He reminded me of this at each turn, particularly when he noticed my focus faltering, or my gaze settling on one woman or another. I rebelled, of course, falling desperately in love with a ballet dancer a few years later. She was graceful, lithe, and as busy as I with preparations for a career in a competitive, athletic field.

We stole away when we could, and I promised we would find ways to stay together, even when the Olympics took me to other countries, even when practices took up eight or more hours a day, even when her own career took off, and her company toured the world.

It did not work, of course, but it was not I who ended it. And as I was very young and still very emotional, I swore away the notion of love forever, choosing instead to focus only on what would get me closer and closer to my goals as an elite athlete.

I do not know what it is about this woman. Scarlett. Red Rocket. I know basically nothing about her. She seems young, but there is also a wariness to her, a mask that disguises pain or loss or some other life experience that changed her in some way. She has an old soul inside her youthful and beautiful body. I find her intriguing. But what truly surprised me was how angry she seemed about missing our dinner together. That she's looking for something long-term when she's so young. Does that mean she saw me as someone worth considering a longer-term liaison with?

Finishing my drink, I toss a tip on the bar and follow her, seeing her long legs topped by her green skirt retreat around a corner and onto an elevator. I watch the numbers until the car stops, and then I push the button to follow her. When I make my way into the fifth-floor bar and scan the room, she's sitting at the counter, alone.

Fucking perfect.

It is easy to watch her, to become transfixed by her. She is an incredibly beautiful woman. Her hair, such a sensuous color. Her skin, so fine with just a smattering of pale freckles I noticed earlier when I was being a creep (her words) by smelling her. I wonder if she has freckles like that anywhere else on her body. Her figure is perfection, with a tiny waist accentuated by lush curves above and below. It is a miracle that no one has put a ring on her finger. She does not fit the profile of a girl who stays single for very long.

I know the reality. She has my attention now, and while she fears a one-night experiment, I fear the opposite. I want her badly—and unfortunately, I know what this means. I will never be able to limit it to one time. If I have her, I'll want her again. And again. I'll linger for one more kiss, one more touch, one more time lost in her.

But for that to ever happen, I will have to gain her trust. I'll have to offer more of myself than I am sure even exists because I shut that door so very long ago. I'm not sure I know how to connect anymore.

As I approach, she looks up from her phone and glowers at me.

The bartender looks to me for an order, so I order two shots of Kauffman and a beer. After he pours the shots, I pick one and hold it up. She makes a dissatisfied face but obliges me, taking the other shot and holding it opposite mine.

"I apologize for standing you up, Red Rocket," I say with a tilt of my head. "I am not good with people, but I would try to be better for an opportunity to get to know you."

She pushes her lips to one side, sighing as she considers what I've said. Then she tosses back the shot and orders another round. As we raise our glasses a second time, she says, "I accept your apology, Viktor, thank you."

Satisfied that this means I am now welcome in her presence; I take the stool next to hers.

"So what part of Russia did you grow up in?" she asks, picking a few bar snacks from a nearby bowl and popping them into her mouth.

"Saint Petersburg."

"Is your family in Russia?"

"Yes. My mother. I have one sister who lives with her husband and children. Galina's husband is a doctor for the German army so they have lived in many places. Right now in Berlin."

"And you played hockey since you were little?"

"Yes. I began instruction when I was three years old."

"Did you play professionally there, too?" she asks.

"Yes. KHL and Russian national team for the Olympics."

"Did you play in Sochi?"

"Yes. Also in Korea where Russia took gold."

"Oh my God, you have a gold medal?"

I nod in the affirmative, content to leave the conversation of my past career behind when she stops her onslaught of questions abruptly. She takes another handful of bar snacks, followed by a long draw from her beer bottle. There is something incongruous about how she looks, drinking from an amber bottle in her fine dress, with her hair tightly managed in a style that confounds me.

I want to unwind all that hair from its prison.

Scarlett notices my staring and her skin flushes down her cheeks to her throat. Another place I want to kiss and caress, her neck. God, I want my lips on her neck so badly. I adjust my position on my seat, as my cock has come to stiff attention. She called me creepy earlier. Surely, having an erection in a public place such as this would only add to her assessment of me.

There is a long silence between us. She looks me over and also at her phone periodically. Finally, she says, "You're supposed to reciprocate. Ask about me."

Oh. I suck at this. I do want to know more about her, which is a shock in itself. But since I've been in America, not many have asked me about me. Especially the women I've encountered. Will she reject me because of my inability to converse properly? *But I have to try.*

"Where did you grow up?" I sound like an idiot as I ask the question.

"Here."

"In this hotel?"

She gives me a vague, indulgent smile. "No. Not in this hotel. In Las Vegas."

"I was not aware that people grew up in a town like this."

"They do. Babies are born here every day. Evan and Holly's baby was born here."

"Yes, of course." Though I had not given a single thought to the child of Evan Kazmeirowicz prior to this moment. It seems just yesterday we were brawling in a nightclub. Now he is married, a father, a team captain. He is a completely different man.

"You don't like him very much, do you?"

"I don't dislike him. I am indifferent to him. He is a teammate. And he did not finish at his best this season. Had he been playing to his best ability; we would have won that final game."

She purses her lips, eyes narrowing. "So, your bonehead penalty had nothing to do with it?"

"He did not score even once in that game. Both Crush goals came from defensemen. This is unacceptable," I explain. "He is paid very highly to score many goals."

She lets out a light laugh and sits back. "That's the most animated I have ever seen you before, Viktor Demoskev."

"This is hardly important; I speak only facts."

"You have a hard time admitting when you've messed up, don't you?" With a smug grin, she takes another long pull on her beer before slamming it on the bar and ordering herself another.

"I have been told that before, yes."

She starts to comment, but before she can say anything, two young women come up, asking if I am Viktor from the Crush.

I nod and they ask to take selfies with me. I sigh, ready to tell them I don't sign autographs or take pictures with fans, but they have their phones out before I can stop them. I must look like a deer in the headlights. I know I must have no expression on my face. But they both kiss me on the cheek and thank me, running off to their group once more.

After this nonsense, I regain my focus on the beautiful Scarlett and find her staring at me with the tiniest, most amused smile on her face.

Scarlett

VIKTOR DEMOSKEV HAS HAZEL EYES. I wish I could examine them in natural light, but I think they're gray and blue and green and even a little yellow. I wonder how someone ends up with such eyes. He also has a deep scar high on his right cheek. I don't have to wonder how he got the scar, however. This man has fought in endless battles on the ice for most of his life, and scars are just a part of playing professional hockey. It's surprising really that he doesn't have more visible scars than just the one.

"Scarlett, what is your family name?" he asks, trying to pretend he didn't just have two blitzed puck bunnies slobber all over him.

Family name? What the heck is a family name? Oh, last name, maybe? "It's Woods."

"Oh." He frowns slightly. "I thought it might be Irish."

"Because of the red hair and the green eyes?"

"Yes."

"Got it from my mom. She was an O'Shea. My dad was a boring old Woods."

"Was? They have passed on?"

"My mom has passed, yes. She died of cancer when I was in middle school. My dad? Unknown. He disappeared. He had some gambling debt so he may be at the bottom of the ocean. Or he could be drinking frilly beverages under a beach umbrella on a private island in witness protection. Who knows?" I lift a shoulder, trying to keep it light. Viktor doesn't need to know how much I've worried about the whereabouts of my father for the last two-plus years.

"My English is not strong enough to follow all of that. You speak quickly." His brows furrow in concern, I think? Hard to tell what his minimal facial expressions mean. They're all kind of similar.

"I'm kinda drunk. The speed of my speaking increases tenfold after my fourth beer."

Viktor just looks down at the bar, then takes a swig of his beer, seemingly unable to figure out how to respond to such an assertion. I take the time to study his profile. It's a good one. He's so, so sexy sitting on the barstool beside me. He's got this light blue, button-down shirt on, unbuttoned at the neck. It's untucked, looking nice but relaxed, like he didn't care enough to tuck it in and knew he'd look all the sexier for it. I can see why those girls were kissing on him, even so, he didn't appear to be interested in their attention. Viktor doesn't have a reputation for sleeping around as opposed to some of the players on the team. His private life is pretty locked down. I wonder if maybe he doesn't know how to flirt. Or maybe he doesn't have much experience with women in general. But somehow it seems impossible that an elite athlete Olympian pushing thirty hasn't spent the last decade bouncing puck sluts on his "hockey stick" at ice rinks all over the world.

I wonder what he'd do if I just lifted my skirt and started to ride him right here. Crowd be damned. Let's have some drunk, public fornication. That wouldn't get me fired or anything.

I giggle to myself. I am a little drunk. I need to stop imbibing and maybe eat something. Now there's a very good idea.

And, oh, there are two creepy-looking dudes in suits at that booth over there. And they're staring at us both. I wonder if they're in the mafia with Viktor? I should just ask him if he's in the Russian mafia, right? Just get it out in the open and know for sure? I can't sleep with a guy who's in the mafia. Can I?

I mull this over while we sit in awkward silence.

Viktor is not a good conversationalist. Why does the word conversationalist make me think of cunnilingus? Maybe he's better at that than at the talking? That would be on the plus side of things for us to hook up.

Oh, goodie. Here comes his weird agent.

The slithery guy with the slicked-back hair and gold tooth steps up and claps Viktor on the back that same way he did at the game. "Viktor! This is the second time I have found you with this young lady. I must have an introduction." He gives us a jovial smile, gold tooth winking like an eye back at me. Yeah, that's not the least bit creepy...

"This is Scarlett Woods, who works in promotional media for the Crush. Scarlett, this is Vlad Nechaev, my agent." I sense irritation from Viktor but it's hard to know for sure.

"Hi," I say, just as the two goons get up and head our way.

They're friggin' huge, and both are carrying briefcases. Who carries a briefcase into a bar? That's just really shady.

Vlad says something to Viktor in Russian, followed by, "Just join us upstairs for a few moments."

Viktor grits his teeth but gives a short nod. He turns to me and says, "I am sorry to be interrupted. I have business upstairs."

"It's fine," I tell him. "See you around."

He stands and all four men leave. I immediately grab my phone and send a text to Pam.

> Scarlett: I'm having the WEIRDEST night.

> Scarlett: Very strange interactions with Viktor.

> Scarlett: I should run fast, and far, far, far away.

Pam: Where are you? Get your ass back up here.

> Scarlett: I need food. Having some sent to the suite.

> Scarlett: Be back after the spins go away.

Pam: You better!

I can't be happy with just my text to Pam, though. No, I need to get Viktor out of my head. I think about cute Sid, the photographer. Why isn't that guy here? Maybe he should be. I got his number when we were doing those shots at the championship game. You know, in case we needed to talk about work. Hee hee.

> Scarlett: Siddy. I'm at Pammy's party. You should be here too.

Sid: Siddy?

> Scarlett: New name for u.

Sid: Nope. No like.

Scarlett: Sid-bear? Sexy Sid?

Sid: LOL. No.

Scarlett: Okay. Just Sid. Come to LINQ?

Sid: Wasn't invited. Not a crasher.

Scarlett: Be my gate.

Scarlett: No. Be my sate.

Sid: LOL

Scarlett: BE MY FUCKING DATE. There!

Sid: So, you've had a few tonight, have you?

Scarlett: Only five beers and two shots. But my phone wasn't playing nice. Come on, Sod, be my date.

Sid: Sod?

Scarlett: SID!!!

Sid: I think your bed and a cup of water needs to be your date right now.

Scarlett: Burned. I'm sad now.

Sid: Sorry to disappoint.

Sid: Text me undrunk sometime.

Scarlett: Fine.

Fine. Even Sid doesn't want to be with me tonight. Viktor could have stayed with me, but nope. A meeting with his sinister Mafia friends. Meeting. Schmeeting. There is nothing appealing about this drunken gal, that's for certain. Hot Russian hockey player sniffing episode aside.

Yep. Looks like I've hit my limit. I need food. All will be better if I can get some hot fries in my face.

I manage to not fall off the stool, pleasantly surprised that Viktor somehow cleared my tab for me. That was nice of him. He's definitely growing on me since he faced the music and apologized, possible mafia connection notwithstanding.

But I am on a mission right now and only one thing will do.

I need French fries.

Stat.

10
the mafia? really?!

Viktor

Vasily releases the tourniquet from my upper arm and slips the needle from my vein, placing a cotton ball over the tiny hole. He hands me a plastic cup and nods his head toward the bathroom where Oleg awaits to watch me piss for the millionth time.

"*Tebe nravitsya moy chlen*?" Which means, "Do you like my dick?"

"It is same as last time I saw it," he says, humorless.

"Pissing in cup is same as last time. Same as always," I say. "Clean piss. No drugs."

He lifts his shoulders. "Not my problem."

"Why must we do this?" I know the answer. I always know the answer, but it is fucking stupid. Vlad does not trust the American officials to be honest about my results. He thinks they have something against Russians and will accuse me of using performance-enhancing drugs even if I have not. He wants to send these samples back home so that we have independent, Russian confirmation that I am clean. Just in case.

I zip up, wash my hands, and head back out to the room, where Vlad flips through television channels as he waits.

"Done?" he asks.

I nod and roll my eyes.

"Good boy. Summer league starts next month, and you will have Olympic training early next season. It will be a busy year."

"It would be good to have a second Olympic gold and a cup," Oleg says. "Otherwise you piss so many times for nothing."

Vasily laughs at this. "No cup or gold if your face is in red-haired pussy."

"Do you think the hair of her pussy is also red?" Oleg asks.

This makes my blood boil. I cannot allow these two idiots to talk about Scarlett in this way. I growl at them in warning, my hands balling into fists.

"Leave him be," Vlad says. "If he wants to fuck a little redhead, that is fine. He will leave soon anyway to focus on the ice once more."

I suppose he is right. I will be leaving for the summer. It is not good to be so focused on a woman I will not see again until fall. She wants something serious. I cannot provide that, even if I wanted to.

"Well, walk us down to the lobby?" Vlad asks.

"We can talk about your training schedule up until you leave for Russia?"

I follow the men out, listening to Vlad's suggestions. I don't really need him to play personal trainer. He has probably never worked out a day in his life. But I listen and nod, pretending I'm listening. When I step back into the elevator, I've already returned to thinking about Scarlett. So, it is almost as if I have conjured her when a ping sounds on floor number five and she stands waiting as the door opens.

"You!" She points as she steps into the metal box with me.

"Hello, Red Rocket. Where are you heading?"

"To go do some work for the Las Vegas Crush." She is slurring her words and it is adorable. "Very important work. I'm very busy with important work to do."

My eyebrows rise into my hairline. I nearly smile. She is very, very drunk.

"Who were those guys? Why were they carrying briefcases? Were they carrying drugs? Money? Guns? Are those guys in the mafia? Are you in the Russian mafia, Viktor?"

I am not sure how to answer these questions. I just say, "They are my agent and hockey officials. No one to worry about."

"Bullshit."

"And bullshit to you, too. You are not working. You are drunk."

Scarlett peers at the row of numbers and punches in her floor she needs. She gives me a look and steps closer, her finger jabbing at my chest.

"You are very strange, Viktor. I don't know who you think you are but I'm not hanging out with a guy who's in the mafia."

I grab her wrist and pull her to me, leaning down until my lips are nearly touching hers. My words are very clear.

"I am *not* in the mafia."

Scarlett

MY, OH, MY. Viktor has a very deep voice...and very pretty lips.

I still totally think he's mobbed-up. But I don't care because he just denied it in the sexiest tone ever. It was almost animal, like a growl, and when he talks all gruff like that to me it turns me on something fierce.

I should not kiss him. I should not.

But his lips are on mine before I can pull away. His big hand encircles my wrist as if I'm made of twigs. I feel very small around him. And I'm not really all that small.

His tongue is in my mouth, his free hand on my ass. I lift a leg like a dog, pushing my crotch against his. I'd be embarrassed if I wasn't so horny. He pushes me against the wall of the elevator, his kiss so scorching, the feel of his growing cock between my legs so good, I'm helpless to resist.

The elevator pings and we break apart. It's my floor. I literally run away, off the lift and down the hall. Because I am too drunk. He better not follow me…

I hear him call out behind me, "See you very soon, Red Rocket."

11
james bond room service

Scarlett

o, you will not!

Not gonna happen. Nope.

Geesh, what was I thinking, letting him kiss me like that? And humping him like an animal in heat. What was that fresh hell with Viktor in the elevator?!

I have had way too much to drink. I'll just boil it down to being dumb-drunk and file it away in the "never to be thought of again" drawer. It's not that it wasn't hot. To be honest, it was scorching. Viktor is a good kisser. An intense kisser, which is no surprise, since he is intense all the time.

But first, I need to order some food. "Why doesn't this key card work? Maybe I can't stay in this suite, after all? No, there it goes. A happy green light means I can go inside. Yay! Greasy, deep-fried food would be best. I might have a thing for French fries when I'm drunk. I mean, they're good on a normal day, but it's like unicorn food when I've had too much to drink. I don't know why." I also don't know why I am talking to myself about myself and drunk food. *God, this is bad. So used to talking to yourself that you do it out loud too now? Pathetic.*

Food ordered, I plop on the couch in this big-ass suite that I could never afford on a normal day, turn on the television and note with some embarrassment that it's only like eleven at night. It's not nearly late enough for me to be this intoxicated. I need to eat some alcohol-absorbing food, sober my ass up, and get back to that party. I'm not even sure I spoke to Pam tonight. Yikes. Better send her a text.

Scarlett: Waiting on room service. Need fries, stat!

Pam: Somebody did the shameful "drunk too early" thing?

Scarlett: If by "somebody" you mean me, then yes.

Scarlett: Not falling down drunk but def needed a break. Back up soon.

Pam: K. Don't fall on Viktor's dick on your way back. HAHAHAHA

Scarlett: Speaking of which...

Pam: ??!!

Scarlett: I *may* have smooched him in the elevator.

Pam: WHAT?!

Scarlett: He left with big dudes carrying briefcases. Then I ran back into him when they were gone.

Pam: And the smooching?

Scarlett: Long story. Also, we may have rubbed crotches.

Pam: Holy hell!

Scarlett: Be up soon.

Pam: Give me details!

Scarlett: Stop texting me. Go back to your guests!

Pam: That's just pure evil.

While I wait for my food, I flip through the channels and land on some movie about the mafia. It gets me thinking about those guys in suits again. There was no good reason for those guys to be in that bar, eyeballing Viktor, leading him off to do "business." Certainly not at ten o'clock at night while Viktor's supposed to be at a friend's engagement party.

What was inside those briefcases? It really kills me, not knowing. Thinking back on the game, it occurs to me that Viktor, a very experienced player, did a very dumb thing at a *very critical point* in the championship game. I wonder…

Is it possible he threw the final game on purpose? Maybe that was cash, his payoff in the briefcases?

My eyelids start to get heavy. I need to fight sleep so I can go back to the party. What kind of lightweight leaves a party so early?

A sharp knock at the door wakes me up. I hop to my feet and head for the door. Thank God room service was quick tonight. No forty-minute wait for me.

Opening the door, the room-service cart is there, but...what is he doing here? In a full tuxedo, holding a bouquet of flowers. What the heck is Viktor doing here? I look out and down both ends of the hallway, expecting a camera crew or to see the hotel staff hanging around, or something. But the hallway is quiet. It's just me and the big, hot, sexy, Russian who ticks every one of my erogenous boxes.

And he's brought my fries. Let's not forget about those. I grab the cloche-covered plate and head back in the room, singularly interested in my delicious-smelling duck-fat fries. Yes, I know what a cloche is. I work as a server. Duh.

I hear an honest-to-goodness chuckle as Viktor wheels the cart into the room behind me. "No tip?"

I'm too busy shoving food in my face to do more than just grunt in response. I'm sure I look quite ladylike, sitting on the couch in my cute dress, ramming fries in my mouth like a starving bear.

Viktor shoves his hands in his pockets and heads

over to the large row of windows looking down on the Strip. "It is a nice view from here."

I switch the television to the music channels until it lands on some soft jazz music that fills the strange silence in the room. I take a few more bites as I study his silhouette against the window. The view of Viktor in a tux on display for me to stare at to my heart's content is indeed a "nice" one. He fills out his bespoke tuxedo very nicely...indeed. Arms crossed; the flexing of his biceps tightens the fabric of his jacket sleeves while he appreciates the view of nighttime Vegas.

I shake myself out of my shameless gawking and stand up, testing my sobriety before slowly walking over to him.

"Yes," I agree. "I grew up here, but the view never gets old."

A long silence stretches between us. Why is it so hard to make small talk with this guy?

"So, you're all dressed up." He was in a nice, button-down and jeans earlier. He looked sexy in that, but in a tux? He looks spectacular. Viktor is quite the snappy dresser as I've noticed in pre-game press videos of players arriving to the arena dressed in their suits per the NHL dress code. All the guys have no choice really. But some pull it off better than others. Viktor's tux is European cut and he looks freaking delicious in it.

"You look so lovely in that dress, I felt I should,

what do they say? Turn up my heat? Heat up the game?"

I let out a laugh at this. "I think you've combined two sayings, 'turn up the heat' with 'up my game.' Which you did. You look like James Bond."

"I think that is good? Yes?"

I can't help the wide smile I know is on my face. "Yes, it's good."

"Excellent." His expression has lost the hardness it usually has, but still not anything close to a smile.

"You just happened to have a tuxedo lying around your hotel room?"

"I brought several options. I don't go to parties like this one often. I was not sure what the dress code would be."

"It's Vegas. Anything goes."

"I think I understand your meaning."

"I mean, you could show up in your underwear and no one would probably think a thing of it."

He looks perplexed, his nose wrinkling kind of cutely as he considers going to a party in his underwear. "I don't think that this would be good for me...because I am not wearing underwear."

I nearly choke with shock, laughing out loud at this admission. My reaction must amuse Viktor because his lips quirk. It's a smirk, maybe? Not a full smile, certainly. I am not sure if he's even capable of those. But it's a look of amusement, anyway. I think Viktor just made a joke, though. It's a breakthrough!

"We should probably go back up to the party," I suggest.

"I don't want to go back to the party." He holds out a hand for me to take. "I would rather stay here with you, Red Rocket."

I bite the corner of my bottom lip. The squiggly haze of too many drinks has dulled. I see more clearly now, the flecks of color in his eyes. The softness of his lips. The sharpness of his features. "What would you like to do if we stay?" I ask as I put my hand into his.

My question is heavy with implication. The whole vibe around us has changed from light and jovial to hot and dark. I know I should say no. I totally should. And I try to say no, I really do. But instead I hear myself asking, "You didn't put on that tux just to hide out in a hotel room, did you?"

He's still holding my hand. My heart is pounding and roaring in my ears, but I think he says, "I put on this tux only to take it off again."

I'm pulled to Viktor, my head only hitting the hard wall of his chest because he's so tall. He wraps an arm around my waist, still holding my hand. He starts to move, just slightly, and I realize he's trying to dance with me. It's a little shocking, something I never would've expected from him.

"I have not done this in a very long time."

"Dancing?"

"Courting," he corrects. "Dancing. Talking.

Touching. Kissing. Fucking. I have not done any of it in a long time."

Well then…

I won't be a cliché. I won't be the girl who balks and says she's not that kind of girl. I am that kind of girl. I am not afraid of sex. I enjoy it. Even though I haven't had any in a long time.

Either.

I haven't wanted some quick, drunken hookup. I want to make a connection with someone who wants the same thing. And even though I thought Viktor would just want a quick hookup, now I'm not so sure. I don't know exactly what he's looking for—not yet—but I feel certain it's not something meaningless. I could sense a great deal of honesty in his words.

Frankly, I'm not sure it matters anyway. The way he just said *fucking*? Straight down to my core it went. Holy hell.

"You're very direct, Viktor."

"There is no point in playing games, Red Rocket."

"My name is Scarlett." It comes out kind of breathless. How embarrassing.

"Scarlett. A name as red as your hair. Beautiful."

"It was there when I was born. Word is that my mother saw all that red and picked my name on the spot. My father thought it was too literal but—"

He stops my babbling with a kiss.

Thank God.

Why were we even talking at all?

His kiss is gentler than the one before in the elevator. Just his soft lips on mine, but my hands find their way to his nicely stubbled cheeks as I push myself closer. My mouth opens from his tongue pressing for access. He takes possession of my mouth at the same instant his hands grip my ass to pick me up. Which he does effortlessly—my skirt pushing up my hips as I wrap my legs around his torso for support.

His lips move to my jaw, my neck. Gooseflesh raises on my skin; it feels so good. I let out a sigh of want. Viktor responds by walking us into the bedroom and laying me down on the large bed. The white duvet is soft, a puff of air escaping as my weight settles down into the fluffiness. I feel so swept away in the moment. As if I am unable to say no or steer us away from what will happen.

And I *know* without a shadow of a doubt what is going to happen here with this man in this room tonight.

Sex. Some really dirty, hot, kinky, sex.

"Take your hair down." Four small words delivered in a commanding tone that requires nothing but my compliance. God, he does not waste time with unnecessary words. Or maybe it's just *how* he says them. To me.

It takes a moment to find all the pins and undo the braids, but the look on Viktor's face as he watches my hair unravel to splay out on the white duvet is totally worth it. That tiny smile is there at the corners of his lips again, but his eyes have gone dark with want.

"That's it, Scarlett." Then he says something in Russian. I have no idea what, and he doesn't translate for me, but it sounds dirty. I like it. A lot.

"What now?" I ask, my chest heaving from my breasts ready to push out of the top of my strapless dress.

"Roll over." It's another order, not a request.

I roll to my stomach, nervous with anticipation as Viktor puts a hand on my ass before sliding it up to the top of my zipper. I shiver as he pulls the zipper all the way down in one single move. He finds the hem of my green dress and tugs down sharply. My dress is no match for his determination and strength. It obeys without protest and lands on the floor with a swish. I'm left shivering in the cool air with only my black thong for a covering.

"On your knees, Red Rocket. I want your pretty ass in the air."

I do it without hesitation.

And then just the tips of his fingers make contact with the exposed skin of my backside. I'm so worked up I forget to breathe as I wait for what he'll do next. But then he hooks a finger under the slim fabric along the crack of my ass, pulling it down, baring everything I have to his eyes. I'm totally naked.

He makes a sound that can only be termed a growl. And again, he speaks Russian words that make me feel like I might combust. I push toward him, needing to feel his touch.

He has one hand caressing my hair but that's not what I want right now. A whimper escapes my throat. He responds with a sharp tug on my hair in tandem with a cracking smack of his other hand to my ass. *Total caveman in the bedroom too.* And I freaking love it. I moan and clench my thighs together in desperation as I am held captive by my Mad Russian caveman. *Jesus, help me.*

"Use your words, Red Rocket. Tell me what you want."

"I want—I want—to be touched and...fucked."

"Say, please."

"Pleeease, Viktor."

He answers quickly. He dips his fingertips along my pussy, finding me slick and wet. When he presses two fingers inside me, I nearly die it feels so good. Without warning, I sink back onto his hand to push those fingers even deeper. I start to move my hips back and forth, but the bastard punishes me. His fingers disappear along with his touch as his hand retreats.

I groan, terribly frustrated, which just makes Viktor chuckle. He gives me a gentle bite at the back of my neck right behind my ear and says, "I will make this so fucking good for you, Scarlett. Be patient."

He starts the process once again, his fingers

exploring my naked body, my folds, my clit, before finally—thank God—pushing inside me once again. He strokes his long talented fingers in and out with a slow rhythm that works me into a frenzy in no time.

When his mouth joins his fingers, I gasp. I feel so exposed—so naughty—but if he stops, I might die. This man will have my death on his conscience if he stops.

Viktor is very talented with his tongue. He sucks on the skin between my legs, on my sensitive clit. His tongue licks at my arousal before he slides that wicked tool of torture up, up, up to the space between my cheeks. *Oh my God, he did not.* But yes, he did just dip his tongue *there*, in that most forbidden of places, before moving back to where his fingers are busily stroking in and out of me.

My body responds as he picks up the pace, the telltale tingle of one spectacular orgasm building inside me. I let out a noise, guttural, animal, and he suddenly flips me onto my back again. I'm naked, panting, baring my teeth. My legs splayed apart in desperate invitation. I don't even care how I must look to him right now.

"I want to see you when you come," he growls, shoving his fingers back inside of me. "Do you want it hard?"

"Mmmmm," I moan.

"Use your words," he commands.

"Yes," I grind out, my hips now pushing against his fingers insistently. "Yes. Hard. Please."

"Good girl."

In and out. In and out. His fingers plunge into me, hard, fast. My hips push up off the bed, my muscles straining as I thrust my body toward that precipice. My hands grip the soft bed coverings. I shake my head back and forth, the sensation overtaking me as the orgasm rips through me, my inner walls clenching around his fingers, inhuman sounds of pleasure filling the silence around us.

As the orgasm slows, the aftershocks continue. Viktor keeps pumping his fingers in and out, more slowly now, letting me ride the waves until they cease.

My eyes are closed for a long time. Endorphins flow through my body. God, I needed that orgasm more than I ever realized. When I open them, I find Viktor staring at me, his eyes reflecting my own lust right back at me. He gives me just the merest grin before dropping his face down to my pussy again, lapping at the proof of my climax with his talented tongue.

I manage to get out a few words of my own even though it's darn near impossible to speak with him tonguing my clit so expertly. "Get naked, I want to see you."

He pulls away reluctantly. I can tell by his expression. "I find I very much enjoy pleasuring you, Scarlett."

"Great." Sexual satisfaction has made me feel extra confident. "Because I like to be pleasured. But I still want to see you naked. You said you only wore that tux so you could take it off. Your plan worked perfectly. Now take it off."

Viktor

SCARLETT'S HEAVY, creamy breasts hold my attention as I pull off my jacket and tie. Her nipples are pebbled. I've decided to make her come just by playing with those beautiful tits sometime.

Sometime...

I will be gone in less than a month. It's unrealistic to think there will be more time between us after this weekend. But then I think about her words.

"I want something real. I want a real connection. You're just another horny player trying to score for the night. And it's not going to be me!" And yet, here I am. There can't be more. *Focus, Demoskev.* Focus on the time between us right now.

Scarlett's body is perfect. Her curves are gorgeous, her skin is softer than I even imagined. She keeps her pussy closely managed, but there is a small strip of red hair left for me to appreciate. It's beautiful the way she's positioned herself after her orgasm, her legs open, one bent at the knee, allowing me to see... everything. Her clit is swollen, begging for much more attention. Her pussy is slick and wet with the evidence of her pleasure. My mouth and tongue are coated with her scent and taste, which has made my cock turn to iron for wanting her.

I unbutton my shirt as she watches, her eyelids heavy, her tongue tracing her top lip hungrily. When I pull away my shirt, she smiles. It's a flirtatious, sexy smile. Like she knew what she would find there.

"You like what you are seeing, Red Rocket?" I ask as I toe off my shoes.

"Mmm. Ripped abs. Defined pecs. Big biceps. What's not to like?" she asks with a giggle. "But what's under those pants?"

A laugh escapes through my nose, just a puff of air. The unfamiliar tug at my lips starts up again. I am almost smiling. It has been a long time. I unbutton, unzip, and slip the black trousers down so that they pool on the floor at my feet.

"Oh!" is Scarlett's initial reaction. I raise an eyebrow in question. "One, you weren't lying that you weren't wearing anything underneath."

"I was not. And two?"

"Your cock is huuuuugggge!" she yells, laughing. It's a manic, almost nervous laughter. She might still be a little bit drunk.

"Where do you want this cock?" I stroke it slowly as she stares at me.

She puts a hand between her legs, her fingers strumming against her clit. Her hips start to move at the attention, and the telltale sheen of wetness increases from her sweet cunt.

"Let me think," she says playfully. "What about you? You like what you see?"

I nod. "I like the way your breasts fall against your body. I like how heavy they are. I like the color of your nipples."

She takes her free hand and plays at one breast, tweaking the nipple, rubbing the soft skin around it with her fingertips. My cock starts leaking a few drops from the tip. Sweet Scarlett notices, moving the hand between her legs so she can use both hands to push those two gorgeous tits together. "Come get them," she says hoarsely.

I climb on top of her, hovering, positioning my cock between her breasts. The softness of the skin feels good to me, so I push forward and back. Scarlett opens her mouth, her tongue reaching out to taste the head of my cock every time it comes near her mouth.

When she lets go of her breasts, they fall away and I push upward, meeting her mouth, plunging inside. Her tongue swirls around my shaft, toys with my head. She opens her throat so I can fill her more deeply. I hold the back of her head with my hands and guide her mouth on and off my cock. I fuck her mouth deeply until she starts to gag a little. I let up and allow her to settle before going again. The sight of my dick disappearing into her mouth against those dark pink lips of hers is enough to make me come, but I don't want the first time I come with Scarlett to be this way.

It's been so long that I'm not sure how long I can

last. I pull my cock out of her pretty mouth and tell her so, but her reply is, "I don't care." She says the same thing again when I tell her I don't have any condoms. She also mumbles something about a "shot" and thrusts her hips up to grind against me instead. I guess that is the "go-ahead" for fucking. Thank God, because I am desperate to be inside of her. So when I pull away, it earns me a stern protest in the form of a frustrated groan. Scarlett makes a lot of sex noises. Which I like very much. She is very open and animalistic in bed. And I have absolutely no wish to tame her.

I give myself a moment of recovery by exploring her nipples with my tongue and teeth. She arches her back, pushing toward me, her sounds of pleasure urging me to bite harder, suck harder, pinch harder. When I finally push inside her, she falls apart instantly, coming hard a second time around the shaft of my cock as she moans and whines and thrashes her head.

"So sexy...your pussy squeezing my cock so tight. With your skin flushed and your tits shaking as you come. You look fucking gorgeous with my dick inside you, Scarlett Woods."

"Ohhh yesss...dirrrty talllker," she moans as she rolls through the end of her orgasm.

"I'm going to fuck you so hard now. Okay?"

"Hell yes, okay. Yes, fuck me. Fuck me hard. So hard...please."

Needing no other confirmation, I pull back and

thrust roughly into her. I keep a fast pace of deep, hard stokes to which she cries out, but I know it's not from pain. No, she loves me fucking her hard, because she's pulling her legs up and holding her knees, giving me as much access as she can while chanting nonsensical words and sounds. She wants this. Her orgasm never seems to cease, only intensifying as I near my own release.

Just before I come, I roar as I pull out, spraying her pale skin with cum. She lowers her legs and looks at me as if she's in pain. I realize she's still coming. And I'm still hard, so I roll to my back where she wastes no time climbing up to straddle me, impaling herself down hard on my dick.

Yebena mat'! chert.

She rides me throughout her orgasms. Only when she is done does she fall to the side, curling up in the crook of my arm, her head on my chest.

"That was..." she starts to say before a giant yawn takes over.

Some crazy, messy, superb, fucking. "Amazing," I finish for her. But she does not say more. I think she is already asleep.

I allow my eyes to close, as well. We will sort this out later. For now, I just need to sleep with this beauty in my arms and breathe in the air scented from our fucking. As if I could ever forget this night. Or her. Whatever happens, I know I'll remember this encounter with her always.

She burrows into my chest and mumbles

something unintelligible before falling back into sleep. I kiss her hair and tell her we will deal with the rest of it tomorrow—right after I fuck a good-morning orgasm (or two or three) into her and she is utterly content and satisfied. I say it all in Russian, speaking in whispers. She will not understand what I said, of course, but I still want her to hear the words coming from me in my native tongue.

When morning comes, however, I am not able to do any of what I promised.

Scarlett is already gone from the suite.

Scarlett

I CAN'T BELIEVE I did that.

I slept with Viktor Demoskev.

And I liked it. More than I care to admit.

Truth be told, I like him. I do. I know he's awkward and he barely smiles. He can hardly keep up a conversation. He's way too direct for his own good. But he's also very sweet in a caveman kind of way. A gentleman caveman, that's what he is. He's certainly sexy and a filthy talker in bed, and boy, can he make a girl come.

I thought I might never stop, that I might just be in some kind of endless loop of perpetual orgasming. It was tremendously good, but I think it would wreak havoc on my daily life.

I woke up several hours later, well into the wee

hours of the morning, and panicked. I totally panicked. Flakes of dried cum on my skin, my crotch sore from all the fun, and maybe just the teeniest bit dehydrated and hung over—I freaked. I grabbed my clothes—everything I brought to the suite—and made my way down to the lobby, doing a total walk of shame in bare feet, with my hair looking like a crazy rat's nest and my makeup kind of half still on my face from the party.

People probably thought I was a hooker. Yikes.

I grabbed a cab and headed home. Yes, I am incapable of facing my decisions head-on. So, I ran away and went home for a long, hot shower. There were like fourteen text messages from Pam. There was one from Holly and even a couple from Sid, who ended up going to the party after all.

But nope, I didn't answer any of them because I was up in the suite doing it with a member of the Russian hockey mafia!

Warm from my shower, I take two Ibuprofen, down a glass of water, and pull on my fuzzy pajamas before falling into my bed. But of course, I can't fall right to sleep. No such luck. I have to fret about the fact that I totally put my job in jeopardy by screwing a player. And I have to see said player—who I promised myself I wouldn't screw but did anyway—at Pam and Georg's other wedding events for the rest of the week.

Dumb.

Ugh. That's me. Scarlett, who wouldn't know a good decision if it hit her across the face.

I finally feel my eyes droop after an hour of tossing and turning. My last thought, as I fall asleep, is something I say out loud just because I am all alone in my apartment, and I can.

"But those orgasms were totally worth it."

12
ghosted

Viktor

"You seem more unhappy than usual," Tyler says from the lounge chair next to me. "That's saying a lot."

Most of the team is down by the pool right now. When I woke up alone in Scarlett's suite, I checked my phone first to see if she had left a message. She had not, but my teammates were up early, chatting about heading to the pool to plan Georg's bachelor party.

All signs of Scarlett were gone from the room as I walked around. No clothing, no purse, no nothing. Spooked, if I had to guess, but why? From my perspective, we were quite compatible sexually. We were more than compatible. We were combustible.

"Not talking?" Tyler asks. "Fine. Then I'll tell you about the threesome I had last night. These two chicks busted in on the party. They totally knew who we were. I ended up in the pool in my underwear and they both stripped to their underwear. I knew my night was picking up then. Ended up having them both in their room. Woke up with bite marks on my cock. Crazy!"

I puff out my cheeks and let out a sigh. Tyler does love to broadcast his sexual escapades. It is something I would like to train him not to do. "It would not be bad for you to keep such stories to yourself sometimes," I suggest.

He scoffs. "Whatever. At least I'm getting laid. Your dick is gonna fall off if you don't use it soon."

"Who says I have not used it?"

"Well, you never talk about women. Never look at women. Other than that hot chick from Holly's office —your Red Rocket."

"Scarlett."

"Scarlett. Yes. What's up with her? Are you in love?"

"That is stupid. I have barely only met her."

"Your refusal to look me in the eye while you deny having the hots for her tells me you actually have the hots for her," he insists.

"You know nothing." Thank God I do not blush. I would be given away. Also, blushing is for pussies.

"Okay, if you're not into her, then pick one of these bikini-clad babes and go talk to her. Maybe get her in the pool for a hand job."

I roll my eyes in response.

"Fine then," he says. "Then I'll assume the next

wedding we'll be planning will be yours and Scarlett's."

"You are a child," I say, shaking my head. "Marriage is not for me. It is also, likely, not for you."

"It's definitely not for me. No fucking way am I letting someone tie me down. I mean, Evan and Georg obviously got the wife lottery anyway. I'd probably end up with some crazy chick who would fuck my best friend and take me for all I'm worth in spousal support."

"You are not worth much yet," I observe. "Barely out of rookie status. Your paycheck is probably very tiny."

"Your cock is probably really tiny," he shoots back.

I raise an eyebrow.

"Okay, you're a big guy. You have a big cock. Got it," he says, raising both hands as if in surrender.

"Do you ever stop talking?"

"Do you ever get laid?"

"Yes."

"Not a lot, though, I'd guess. Or you'd be a happier man."

I give up. "I got la—I was with someone last night. Are you happy to now know this private business of mine?"

"Hallelujah!" Tyler pumps his fist in the air. "Who were you with? Was it good? Why aren't you happier?"

I shake my head and close my eyes. Perhaps if I pretend to be asleep, he will go away.

"Did she ghost you after?"

I open my eyes, only to narrow them at him as I fold my arms across my chest.

"She totally did," he says, conspiracy in his voice. He lowers his volume and asks, "Was it Scarlett?"

I do not confirm or deny the question, but he makes an affirmative sound, obviously taking my silence as an admission.

Pamela and Holly arrive on the other side of the pool with the wedding planner in tow. Pamela looks ready for the pool, a light, white dress over top of a bathing suit that ties at the back of her neck. Georg is up out of his chair immediately, bounding over to kiss his fiancée on the lips. Evan's wife looks miserable, though. She's in shorts and T-shirt, an overnight bag over her shoulder.

Evan stands and wanders to her. He pulls her to his chest in a hug. He says something to her, and she shakes her head. They talk for a minute before he kisses her chastely on the lips and she walks away. I watch as he rubs his palms in his eyes, then runs a hand over his beard. He looks tired. No, not tired—he looks weary. Not even one year since he was married, and it seems the honeymoon is over.

I point at him and tell Tyler, "That is why you do not get married. Do you see him?"

"He looks like hell. Preaching to the choir, brother. I am *never* getting married. Hell to the no."

Evan looks around and then makes some sort of decision to follow his wife. He's shirtless and shoeless, but he runs off, obviously chasing after her.

In watching this scene unfold, I missed the arrival of my Red Rocket who is now standing by Pamela and Georg. Her long hair is in a ponytail, exposing that pretty neck of hers. Wearing a long blue strapless dress with a beaded belt, she is painfully beautiful.

"I fucking knew it," Tyler says with a laugh as he noted my stare. "You could set her on fire, looking at her like that."

I get up, ignoring him, and walk toward her.

"Good afternoon," I say as I approach.

She meets my gaze, but her expression is almost defiant. It is definitely cold. "Viktor."

"I woke up naked in your room and you were not to be found."

Her cheeks flush at this as she steals a quick look to her right, no doubt checking to see if her friend heard what I just said.

"I know I enjoyed our lovemaking. And by the number and intensity of your orgasms, I believe you enjoyed it as well. Am I wrong?"

"Stop," she hisses, her cheeks very pink.

"Stop what? Stop asking why you left after we shared such an incredible experience together?"

"Stop talking so loudly about what should be private between us."

"Oh. Sorry."

She looks everywhere but at me. "I needed to go home and think. It was an overwhelming night."

"You could have woken me up. I would have driven you."

"I needed to be away from you."

"Did I offend you in some way?" I ask.

"No."

"Then, why did you need to get away from me?"

"Because I felt like...I felt like maybe we rushed things. Like maybe I shouldn't have let things go so far between us."

"We did what our bodies wanted," I answer. "We did what felt good. This is not cause for concern."

"So simplistic in your assessment," she says sourly.

"It is simplistic, but why should it be more?"

"I told you, I didn't want some drunken hookup. I didn't want something quick and meaningless. I wanted to connect. And, for the record, I could lose my job because of this."

"How could you? This is nothing to do with your work."

"Except the team has a policy, meant to keep players and staff apart."

"Stupid policy," I state, folding my arms across my chest.

"I won't disagree with you there." She looks around furtively, still worried someone is listening to us. "And it didn't stop Holly and Pam, but knowing my luck, I'll be the straw that breaks that camel's back. I'll be the one to get fired. And I really need my job with the Crush. I actually like working there."

"I don't understand about this camel," I tell her with what must be a look of confusion on my face.

She lets out a small, humorless laugh and adjusts her ponytail. The action pushes her back straight and her breasts jut forward. I cannot help my eyes from focusing on them, plump and round in the stretchy material of her dress. I can almost recall the taste of her nipples in my mouth and the vision of my cock fucking those lush tits last night. I'd need a repeat of the experience to be sure though.

"Stop staring at my tits."

"I cannot. They are too nice."

"Well, you don't see me ogling your perfectly sculpted, smooth, naked man-chest, do you?"

This makes me smirk. "I think you may have ogled. A bit."

She rolls her eyes at me. "I have to go. I just came over to drop my overnight bag in the suite. I have to work a few hours at my second job."

"Second job? You work two jobs?"

"Yes." She waves me off, which means she doesn't want to talk about it. I think. *American women.*

"Will you be back in time for the group dinner tonight? We are taking Georg for his bachelor party after, but I would like to sit with you during the meal. Would that be okay with you?"

"I'll think about it, Viktor." She sounds unsure. "I just don't—I don't know."

"I hope this is not still about game night. I have said I am sorry. I should have stopped to tell you I needed reflection and isolation."

"It's not about that," she answers quickly. "It's hard to put into words."

"Did you not enjoy our time together?"

"I did," she whispers. "Very much."

"Sit with me at dinner. I promise I will be better at conversation tonight; you will see."

Finally, Scarlett looks me in the eye. There is a bit of sadness there, but I don't sense regret from last night. I need to know what is bothering her, but I've also made plans with Tyler. I take her hand, so small and fine, and place a kiss on the palm. "I will see you later. You are beautiful."

She lowers her eyes and says quietly, "Thank you, Viktor."

I don't want to leave her now.

But I have made a promise. The raised eyebrows and smug grin on Tyler's face, says I don't need to confirm it was Scarlett last night.

"Not a word," I growl as I reach my seat next to Tyler. "Let's go. We need to catch the bookies before the afternoon books close on tonight's MMA and boxing matches."

He chuckles at my discomfort, of course.

We pull on our shirts, grab phones and wallets, and head out into the hot afternoon sun.

"I'm taking Jaeger for the win in tonight's main fight," Tyler says.

"Rodriguez," I answer.

"No fuckin' way!" he yelps. "Rodriguez is not strong enough to beat Jaeger."

"He is and he will. You will see the outcome of that fight that I was right."

"What about Petrovich in the MMA ring?" he asks.

"Yes."

We place our bets and leave quickly, walking back toward the hotel. On the way, I see a floral shop. From the looks of the window displays, it specializes in bouquets for hasty weddings. I know Las Vegas is a place where such things happen often.

After asking Tyler to wait, I step inside, placing a wad of cash on the desk and asking for the nicest roses to be sent to Scarlett in the bridal suite at the LINQ. I do not understand completely what she is thinking, but I do remember my papa giving my mama flowers and how she always smiled with tears in her eyes. *Maybe Scarlett will smile with tears when she sees them.*

She will have to sit with me at dinner now.

13
policy, schmolicy

I did a three-hour shift at the casino to cover for another server. It was shorter than my usual shift, which was nice, and we ended up being busy enough for me to pocket a few hundred in tips, which is also nice.

Now, though, I'm back to overanalyzing my night with Viktor. What the heck was I thinking? Why did I let myself sleep with him? I mean, I know this guy isn't boyfriend material. He's not the guy I'm going to marry. I promised myself I wouldn't do this, wouldn't fall into bed with some random dude, hoping for instant connection or whatever. It never ends well.

I don't know what to feel when I think of Viktor. He's so stiff, so emotionless. Just once, I'd like to see him smile. Really smile. Not one of those tiny little half-grins—the closest I have ever seen him get to anything resembling a smile. The big Russian is a mystery. And something's totally going on with him. It's weird. The guys in suits are strange enough, but I swear I also heard him mention bookies earlier when he and Tyler were talking by the pool.

Yet…he also feels familiar to me. Comfortable. It's an odd juxtaposition, being around him. It feels awkward and sensual *but also* comfortable. I think that's why I feel so conflicted about whatever this is that's happening between us.

See? Totally overanalyzing. He's a big brute of an athlete. He's probably not thinking anything about what this all means and blah, blah, blah. No, he's probably just happy to be able to tell his buddies he scored last night.

And he really did score. *I* really did score. Seriously. Hottest sex I've ever had, bar none. We are quite compatible in the sack. So maybe I'm making too big a thing of it? Maybe we should just get it out of our systems, get off a few more times, and call it a day? Hmm. Decisions, decisions…

I get a text from Pam telling me to come up to her new-and-improved suite, where she's got hair and makeup people at the ready again. I don't have fancy clothes for events like these. I packed a little black dress, but it feels juvenile as I pull it out of my overnight bag. I may need to go shopping tomorrow so I'll have something to wear to the wedding. That stack of cash from today's shift will probably get me, like, a pair of socks or something. Shopping on the Strip is expensive.

"Hey girl!" Pam yells as I walk in the room. She's got a beer in one hand and a big blue dildo in the other.

"What. Is. That?" I can't help snickering.

"Um, a big, fake, blue, dick...obviously," Pam sings before reading aloud from the packaging, "Turn out the lights and illuminate your playtime with Firefly's 8-inch glow-in-the-dark pleasure dildo."

"Oh-kay. And why do you have it?"

"Bachelorette gift from the team. The signed card said it was to make up for Georg's tiny cock."

Everyone in the room howls at this.

"So, Pammy," I say, taking in the vast suite. It's really huge, with a sunken living area, a big kitchen, and a crazy, half-circle view. There's got to be a bedroom somewhere around here, but the main space alone is bigger than my actual apartment. "I am utterly wardrobe challenged tonight."

"Say no more." She hops up and puts the blue dildo on the coffee table. "I've got just the thing."

Ten minutes later, I'm dressed in a black jumpsuit. It's got wide legs, but the sleeveless top part is a showstopper with wide straps and a deep V that goes almost to my belly button. It's very, very sexy, especially when I put on my favorite silver sandals. And what's more, *I feel* sexy. It's something working at a club can scrape away—self-worth. Being felt up, as if it's my job to be leered at. I don't know where Pam had this hiding, but I'm certainly glad she did.

I have the hairstylist just give me a quick blowout,

so my hair is long down my back, smooth and curling just at the ends. The makeup artist gives me a dramatic look, though, to make up for the simplicity of my outfit and my lack of jewelry.

Pam and I are the first ready, while Holly, Devon, and Daisy all take a little longer. I step outside on a private balcony and my friend joins me. She hands me a glass of champagne and we clink our glasses together as we look out on the amazing view of lights and people and the desert beyond.

"So, I need to get this out of my system," I say after a few moments in companionable silence. "I slept with Viktor last night."

Pam doesn't answer. I turn to look at her and find her smirking. One of those "I knew it" types of smirks. *Annoying.*

"How did you figure it out?" I ask.

"Umm, you sent me a text saying you kissed him. You didn't come back and he didn't come back, and today he was staring at you like you were his last meal."

"Well, he can be overly intense."

"But what I want to know is if he was any good, Scarlett." She nails me with a raised brow.

"Amazing." A shiver rocks my whole body as I think about it. "It was mind-blowing. Best ever, bar none."

"Wow, that's a high compliment. Who'd have thought the big dumb rock would know how to use his cock? Oh—I'm a poet!"

I giggle at this. "You're ridiculous. How long have you been drinking today?"

"Since yesterday?"

"Well, you'd better pace yourself, girlie. Can't have the bride wasted at her own party. Also, he's not dumb, I don't think." My oddly defensive feelings for Viktor surprise even me. "His English is very formal at times but he has a good command of it, even if he doesn't always understand American slang or euphemisms. And if you talk too fast, forget it. But he is in no way dumb."

"Sorry," Pam says, putting up a hand in apology. "You're probably right. He's just not very emotive, you know? Hard to tell what's going on in that pretty head of his."

"He's very direct. It's hard to miss what he's thinking about once he opens his mouth though."

"I sense you're not happy about this development?" Pam asks.

"I'm not unhappy. But I can't put my finger on why this sets me on edge. My job, maybe? The policy?"

"Policy, schmolicy, Scarlett." Pam wags a finger at me. "They didn't fire me, and I had near-sex with Georg on my own therapy table at work."

"That's not something I'd broadcast, friend."

She shrugs. "Whatever. We're getting married!"

"That's part of it, too. I can't get too close to him because he's leaving for the whole summer. I won't see him until the fall. And he's got something going on with those bizarre suit dudes. It's shady and I don't like it."

"I don't know," Pam says with a big sigh. "I don't know much about Viktor, but I think you should do whatever your heart tells you. I did and I am soooo happy."

I realize this conversation is going nowhere. Pam needs to eat and see her beloved Georg. But as we step back inside to see how everyone is coming along, I think about her advice. *You should do whatever your heart tells you...*

The problem is I just don't know what my heart is telling me to do yet.

A knock at the door announces the delivery of a huge—and I mean ginormous—spray of red roses. There's other flower deliveries already in the room, many of them from friends in honor of the couple's nuptials. Right on the heels of the floral delivery, Pam's wedding planner enters and announces, "It's time we should get downstairs."

Through the din of excitement and commotion, Pam directs the delivery guy to set the vase on the kitchen counter without checking the card. Pam seems excited, making a beeline for the door. Everyone follows along and we head down the hall to the elevator.

Daisy and Devon chat about a recipe book that Devon is writing. Holly seems in a better mood, looking pretty in a slim-fitting purple dress. She certainly doesn't look like she's had a baby. She's chattering about the guys' plans for the evening. They're doing a bachelor party and she's positive they'll end up at a strip club.

"Who cares," Pam says. "Let them have a little fun. He'll come home to me, and that's all that matters."

"I'm just…Evan used to do that stuff all the time before we got together but…"

"It'll be fine," Pam insists. "Seriously. That man is in love with you like no man has ever been in love before. He's not looking for some side-action. No way."

"I just feel so puffy lately. And emotional. He's got to be so sick of my moods."

"He loves you," Pam says again. "For better or worse, remember?"

"If you were married to Tyler, I might worry," I chime in, trying to lighten the mood.

Holly laughs out loud at this. "No joke," she says. "I wouldn't be surprised if he had like six love children out there in the world. He seemingly has nonstop sex, as that's all he ever talks about."

Devon joins the conversation. "I saw our boy wonder down at the pool earlier. He and the big Russian were ogling and being felt up by women all afternoon. Well, when they weren't heading off to the sports betting joint."

"Sports betting?" I ask. My stomach drops.

"They were blabbing about MMA fights or boxing or some nonsense. Stupid boys."

We don't talk more about this, but it sticks with me for the whole ride down to the restaurant. I can't be with another gambler. I simply can't. Gambling ruined my Stephen's life. My dad's life. It continues to plague *my* life.

Only bad things come from betting. I have learned it over and over and over again. I can't do it anymore. I don't care how hot Viktor is, how great he is in bed. We're done. You'd think I'd be worried about women ogling Viktor or strippers enticing him, but I can't. Nothing will tempt me toward Viktor now.

As we step into the restaurant, Pam's wedding planner stops us and tells us that we need to stick around after dinner. Apparently, Pam and Georg want to do a flash mob at their wedding, and we'll do a practice session right after we eat.

I scan the room and pick out Viktor at the bar with the rest of the guys. He stands out in a crowd, normally, so it's not difficult to find him. Searching him out in public is something I've been doing ever since he joined the Crush, actually. Always from afar, of course. That's my own dirty little secret though. Nobody knows...I don't think. Well, Pam maybe knows. I might have blabbed to her once after a night out on the town.

He looks so fine in his dark blue suit (probably custom) that my eyes literally hurt looking at him right now.

Because even if he was giving thought to something more than a night of sex with me, we were done.

So. Not. Fair.

14
no charity case here

I have worn my best suit tonight. It was custom-made for me by the very best tailor in Saint Petersburg. When I arrive in the bar, I see that I made the right choice. My teammates are also dressed in suits.

Secretly, I do not care to fit in. I'm not bothered when I don't. But I want Scarlett to think I look handsome. She's conflicted about our intimacy last night, but I want her to want me again.

We all toast to Pamela and Georg. He seems genuinely happy and I'm happy for him. There was a time when I considered him a friend, followed by a period when we hated each other. Now, we are on the same team and I respect him. It feels right to be here to celebrate with him.

The men chatter about the bachelor party later, but my eyes scan the edge of the room. I'm rewarded when the women arrive, but Scarlett is the only one who catches my attention. She is the most beautiful woman I've ever known—especially in the outfit she's wearing that seems to have been made to conjure up sinful dreams. My cock twitches in my trousers just from taking in her silky hair, her beautiful face, her sexy body. If I saw her on a movie screen, I would be smitten. I feel like a young boy with a crush. Actually, it's a strange sensation for me to be having at all. It feels unfamiliar to be so… needy for one woman's attention. But God, I want hers.

We are all ushered to a private table and I make sure to get the seat next to her. She gives me a small, private smile but says nothing. I try to engage her, asking her about her day.

"I had to work my second job," she says. "Nothing exciting."

"Where do you work?"

"At the Tangiers, serving drinks. It's terrible work but I make good tips."

I've been inside that casino and I know what the cocktail waitresses wear to work. They show a lot of skin, as is the case for most casinos. Scarlett in such a uniform would indeed make her *very good tips*. The idea of men ogling her sexy body and thinking filthy thoughts makes me feel irrational at best, and murderous at worst. "Why do you require this second job of serving at a casino?"

"I don't make that much working for the Crush and I have to support myself," she says sharply. "Not everyone is rich enough to rent out a hotel for a week."

It feels like a slap in the face, though I know she means the bride and groom. "If you need help with money, I could—"

"Stop." She makes a face of disgust. "I'm not a charity case."

"I just—"

"I know. You're an earnest, direct guy. You make loads of money. And I realize you're trying to help, but I don't need it. So just stop."

"All right. Okay. I'll stop." One battle at a time.

We talk with others at the table through our meal. She barely speaks to me unless I address her directly. She never mentions the flowers I sent. Could they have offended her? Perhaps they were too much? Tyler thought they were too much, and perhaps he was right. It's possible she simply did not like them. Don't all women enjoy receiving flowers though?

Her posture is relaxed, and she doesn't seem angry. I can't read her and would really like to ask her directly what she's thinking. I know she wouldn't like it though, with so many people here to listen in to our conversation.

A pianist starts to play as we finish dessert. A few couples get up to dance, so I ask Scarlett if she'd like to dance, as well.

"No, thank you."

"Ahh." I toy with my napkin.

"I would be willing to take a quick walk, though," she says.

I look up and she gives a strange, short smile. I don't miss opportunities though, so I stand and hold out my hand. She doesn't take it. Instead, she stands on her own and leads the way out of the private dining room, through the restaurant, and into the hallways beyond.

We don't go far, as we've been instructed to stay close for "rehearsal" of a dance number that we will do at the wedding. I don't know what this entails, but it sounds terrible.

The hallway is much quieter than the restaurant. I wait for Scarlett to speak.

"I need to know about those guys from last night. The ones with the briefcases," she finally says. "And why are you betting on sports?"

Why does she sound suspicious? It's not unusual for Russian sportsmen to have their own testers. Why do these things bother her so much?

"Those men are to do with hockey," I explain. "They have business with me, but it's nothing. No big deal."

"And the betting?"

"It is no big deal," I say again. I don't know what she wants to know about it.

"Stop saying it's no big deal," she explodes. "I know what a big deal gambling can be, and how dangerous these types of guys can be. Don't dismiss my questions. Don't hide things from me!"

Her face is flushed red, and tears start streaming down her cheeks. I reach out but she slaps my hand away. I step forward and take her face in my hands. I try to kiss her. At first, she lets me, but a moment later, she pushes her mouth away.

"Stop," she cries. "Just stop, Viktor. Did you throw the championship game on purpose? Was it part of the betting? Was there money in those briefcases?"

I cannot help but laugh, as this is so ridiculous. "Why would I throw the championship away? I have played hockey for my entire life. I am an Olympic champion. Winning the championship cup or medal is always the goal."

"Well, you still haven't given me an explanation." She angrily wipes her tears away with the back of her hand.

"I do not owe an explanation, Scarlett. My life is my life."

"And I'm just some...what do you call me? Red Rocket? I'm just some rocket you screwed. I don't mean a thing. I don't need to know anything about you other than the size of your cock!"

"You are being crazy."

This is obviously the wrong thing to say, because Scarlett's face goes as red as her hair. She opens her mouth, but before she can respond, there is an announcement for the Kolochev/Jenson wedding party to return to the ballroom for dance training. Scarlett's mouth snaps shut as she rushes past me, retreating.

Chto za khren'.
What the fuck just happened?

15
gloriously bad dancing

Scarlett

I just won't look at him. I'll get through this ridiculous dance practice and I won't look at him and then I'll just go back to my borrowed suite and watch a rom-com and eat pizza and feel sorry for myself. I guess I let myself think maybe Viktor and I had made a connection. In my head, I kept thinking he wouldn't want anything more than sex, but I think my heart said otherwise. And now I just feel really stupid.

The choreography is pretty fun though. *Rhythm is a Dancer* by Snap! is our song. I like dancing. I was actually on my high school dance team. For a little while, I suffered under the delusion that I could be anything or do anything—you know, that thing parents tell their kids while they're still innocent and not jaded by how awful life can be—and assumed I'd be like a Dallas Cowboys cheerleader or something when I got out of high school.

Trying to shake myself out of the funk I feel after my interaction with Viktor, I throw myself into learning the moves. It works, and before long I'm cracking up and having a blast.

"You're missing the show." Pam giggles next to me. "Viktor is a gloriously bad dancer. It's amazing."

I think of him holding me, slow dancing when he came to the suite in his tux, and have to shut off the image by closing my eyes. He was a beautiful dancer that time. I take a deep breath and turn to look, trying to act like I'm not all that interested.

"Oh." I cover my mouth to prevent the laugh that wants to escape. "Oh, God, yes."

Viktor is trying. He really is, but his moves to the fast beat of this song are so robotic and stiff. It's almost painful watching him struggle with the dance. If this goes out on a Snapchat, he'll never live it down.

"How could a guy you described as the 'best ever, bar none' be so bad at dancing?" Pam asks quietly, giggling. "I mean, he knows how to use his hips, right?"

I shove my friend playfully. "I can attest to that yes, he *definitely* knows how to use his hips." I track his awkward movements across the dance floor. "But yeah, that's uh...really...bad."

Just then, Devon walks over to him and says what we're all thinking. "You're so stiff. Jesus, Viktor, would you just relax?"

The guys all laugh and rib him, and a few jokes

float around about stiff body parts. Viktor is his usual stoic self, his lips turned slightly down as he shrugs off their joking. He truly seems unaffected by all the teasing. Gotta give him props for not caring what others think of him. I wish I could be more like that.

Music still plays, and everyone watches as Devon starts giving Viktor "lessons" on how to loosen up. She dances right up on him, her pelvis grinding against his before she turns and lowers herself, twerking, her ass right up against his crotch. Everyone laughs, hoots, and whistles, especially when Devon moves behind Viktor, her hands on his hips guiding him, trying to get him to loosen up.

Several times during this exchange, I notice his eyes flit to me. I bite my lip and look away, feeling sick to my stomach. I shouldn't care about this. There's no reason for me to care. We only slept together. There is nothing between us.

Pam puts her pinkies in her mouth and whistles, turning to me with a wide grin on her face. "Seriously, you've got to see this." But the words, and her grin, die out slowly when she sees me. "You okay?" she asks.

"Something must not have agreed with my stomach at dinner. I'm not feeling well. I'm going to head up to my room and get some rest."

"Oh," Pam says, frowning in a way that seems less angry and more concerned. "Well, that sucks."

"It's not a big deal. I'll catch up with you later."

I leave without another word to anyone, feeling

Viktor's eyes on my back as I walk out of there as quickly as possible without actually running. Which is what I would like to do.

Inside the suite, I put on my pajamas, brush my teeth and hair, and take off my makeup. I'm tired, but as I sink into the bed, I'm reminded that this is where I spent hours learning the chiseled planes of Viktor's well-trained body. His body is a machine, and I learned a lot of it during our time together, my curves melting into his hard muscles.

Vivid images assault me, my body heating, desire pooling between my legs, my nipples hardening into tight peaks. It makes me mad, that the sex was so freaking good. I mean, the way he used his body on me...ugh...so good. And he knew what he was doing too. Why does someone so sexy and so good in bed have to be so utterly wrong for me?

I turn on the television, hoping for a reprieve from these thoughts, but as I stare at the screen, all I really see is him. All I really feel is him. My fingers snake down into the waistband of my sleep shorts, under the thin material of my panties, to find the wetness there. I rub at my sensitive clit, my hips arching instantly. I let my fingers explore slowly, but it's not enough and I'm frustrated. So I get up and head for the shower, turning it on high heat, switching the spray so that it comes out in one, hard stream. I stand in the hot water for a long time, touching my nipples, enjoying the view as they peak into hard nubs under my fingertips, under the spray. I move my attention to my clit, so swollen, as I spread my lips apart and jut my hips forward to meet the spray. It hits my extra-sensitive parts just right and I push into it, the harsh stream of water stinging against my skin as the tingle of climax rushes through my body, down to my toes, up to my breasts.

I find myself pumping against the water, pushing myself to climax as thoughts of Viktor swirl in my head, memories of our night together pushing me closer and closer to the edge. When I come, I see bursts of light, the sensation so strong that I cry out his name, "Vik-tor," on a harsh breath, having to sag against the marble wall of the shower to keep from falling on my ass. That orgasm was just what the doctor ordered. And I will not feel guilty for something I needed so badly.

After drying off, I pull my pajamas back on, put my wet hair into a messy bun, and crawl back into bed only to find a text from Pam, letting me know the girls are all having mani-pedis and watching movies in her suite. I have to admit that sounds really nice, so I make my way back up to the top floor.

"Heyyyy!" Pam yells from her seat. She has her toes in a portable pedicure bath, a young woman working on her feet. "Glad you came up, girlie. Feeling better?"

I nod. I'm too blissed out by my awesome orgasm to care about what was bothering me before. Viktor is a sensual man who can dance with and fuck any woman he wants. And clearly, I don't need him. That last orgasm proved that. There. I am back to normal ready to move forward.

"Good," she says. "There're snacks on the table. Holly's picking out a rom-com to watch. We're going to have a nice, relaxing night while those boys are out being idiots."

Devon and Daisy are sitting on the couch, another hotel staff member giving Devon a manicure while she reads a magazine, commenting on some celebrity gossip to Daisy, who looks like she would rather be anywhere else but in this room.

"Oh," Pam says, "I forgot. Go look at those roses over there."

"Why?"

"Just do it," she orders.

I shrug and wander over to the kitchen counter, where there's a humongous spray of red flowers. A card on the table beside it catches my eye. I see my name first, in a messy, masculine scrawl.

 *Scarlett,*

> *I hope to get to know you better. These are just to show that I am thinking of you, and of our night spent together.*
> *Viktor*

I stifle a giggle. I can hear this in his voice, his heavy Russian accent making the words sound stiff and formal. I feel like such a jerk—these were delivered before dinner. No one even looked at them. I sat next to him, argued with him...and he probably expected me to tell him how beautiful they were.

I turn and find Pam staring at me, a knowing look on her face.

"Stop," I say, wandering over to the couch.

"What?" she asks innocently.

"Who are those from?" Holly asks, finally satisfied with her movie choice.

"Viktor," Pam says, a note of scandal in her voice. "Our Scarlett had a hot night with him instead of partying with all of us last night."

"What?" Holly turns to scrutinize me. "You slept with Viktor?"

"Ugh," I groan, flopping back and covering my head with a pillow.

"Was he good?" Devon asks. "I'll bet he was good."

"She said he was the best ever, bar none," Pam announces for all to hear.

"Damn," Devon curses. "I'm kinda jealous."

Daisy looks patently uncomfortable. "We're making Daisy blush," I say. "I don't want to talk about Viktor."

"Wouldn't it be funny if all the Crush guys married someone on staff?" Holly muses. "Fiona would have a heart attack. She'd be like, *Oh, but the fraternization policy...*"

"Screw the fraternization policy!" Pam yells.

"Or screw the players," Devon amends with a giggle.

"Well, three of us have," Holly says. "Who's next?"

"Find me a good one," Devon answers.

Daisy just shakes her head.

I decide I should probably send a text to Viktor. I owe him an apology.

> Scarlett: I just saw the beautiful flowers you sent.

> Scarlett: Feel like an idiot.

> Scarlett: So sorry for yelling at you earlier.

> Scarlett: We can talk later. But thank you for the lovely flowers.

I try not to be offended when he doesn't respond.

16
what is this snap chat?

Viktor

There is a private room in this club that has been rented out for Georg's bachelor party. It is very dark with red lighting. There is a card table in the middle, and many kinds of chairs and lounges along the walls. Some are hidden in dark spots of the room, unlit, offering privacy.

I am nursing a triple vodka on the rocks. Georg is no longer drinking, so he is not his wild self of the past. He seems happy, though, enjoying the dance of a pretty and petite young woman with short, dark hair.

Tyler is on one of the couches, sprawled out like he is in his own living room, several beer bottles on the floor, two women dancing for him. He puts cash in the thong of one, pulling her closer so that she straddles him where he lies. She giggles at something he says, unhooking her bra, her breasts exposed but for glittery stars pasted over her nipples. She arches her back and wiggles, making her breasts bounce. Tyler runs a finger over her bare skin, and I wonder just how much money he gave her, to allow him to be so close, to touch her like that.

My interaction with Scarlett earlier has soured my mood. I don't understand why she is so intent on knowing my business. I liked fucking her—very much—and I would like to get to know her better, but it seems as if she is trying to know too much about me too quickly. What I do to ensure my place on this team is none of her business. Bets I make in the off-season are none of her business.

I suck down the rest of my drink, trying to blur the strange array of feelings that are connected to this Red Rocket. I order another, as well as a beer. Tyler hoots happily to see me picking up the pace.

"There we go, big guy," he calls from the couch. "This is a party and you all are acting like a bunch of old fucking ladies. Get drunk with me. Put your face in a pair of titties!"

"Shut up, Tyler," I say, but there is no conviction to it. "It is Georg's party. He should have his face in titties."

"Agreed!" Evan hoots.

Our team captain is slightly drunk, more drunk than I have seen him since he has been married. He seems to be drinking for a cause. Perhaps trouble in paradise? It just reminds me of the reasons I do not need or want a relationship. I have not sought out the company of women very often and not for a while. It is enough to manage the expectations of my agent and my team. I am not here to settle down and find a wife. It is obvious that this is not right for me, as the first woman I have shown an interest in has not even acknowledged the flowers I sent. She has tried to control me already. This is not good.

Tyler is suddenly at my side, holding the hand of a thin woman with long, red hair. She is nothing like Scarlett, her hair obviously dyed its fiery color.

"You like redheads," Tyler says before letting out a long belch. "This is Trixie. She has red hair and wants to dance for you. My treat."

"I do not need you to pay for her to dance for me," I grumble, pulling out my wallet.

"No, no," Tyler says quickly, holding out a hand to stop me. "You need to lighten the fuck up tonight. This first one is on me."

I sigh and shrug. Trixie begins her dance and Tyler wanders off to make sure that Georg is being taken care of. It is his party, after all. He and Evan are playing cards at the card table, each of them with a showgirl on their laps.

"Pay attention to me, big boy," Trixie says in a little-girl's voice. "I'll be so sad if you ignore me."

I force my gaze to the young woman. She is petite and rail thin. Not curvy like Scarlett. Her hair is not even real hair. I think it is a wig. She is pretty, I suppose, but I find myself only comparing her to Scarlett.

"You don't like what you see?" Trixie pouts. "You're frowning."

"He always frowns," Tyler yells from wherever he has landed.

I shake my head. "You are okay to look at."

She mirrors my frown. "Well, I'll have to show you something that pushes me past the okay mark and up a notch to attractive or hot."

I shrug again, unsure what to say in response. I shoot back my vodka and go straight to my beer. A pair of shots appear in front of me, and I toss them back quickly. Now the buzz is beginning.

"You can touch me," Trixie says. "Put your hands on my waist.

I do as asked, but thoughts of my night with Scarlett come back to me. I think about texting her but realize I left my phone in my hotel room. I will just imagine this young woman is my Red Rocket. I will keep drinking and allow the haze of alcohol to make me imagine her curves, her long neck, her creamy skin. I will imagine the taste of her warm, wet cunt on my tongue and the way her pussy clenched around my cock as we fucked.

"There we go," Trixie says, smiling as she swishes her ass along my lap, finding my cock semi-hard. "I like to see a little guy wake up."

"Is not little," I grumble.

"Oh, I'll bet it's not," she says, leaning in, speaking quietly. "Maybe you'll show it to me later? Special price and I'll suck you dry."

Perhaps before the night is over, I may take her up on her offer.

As the evening goes on, Trixie shows up several times. The more I drink, the more money I shove into her black G-string. Once, my fingers graze her bare pussy and I find her wet. It makes me hard, even though I am still only imagining Scarlett. Even so, this would be easy. I could fuck her and pay her and there would be no question about suitcases and betting. I could close my eyes and think of Scarlett, ramming my cock into this woman with no worry that she could expect a thing from me the following day.

I drink and drink some more. My teammates, save for the bachelor, drink as well. The party becomes louder. Raunchier. Tyler disappears for a while to the dark corner.

When he returns, finding Trixie wiggling on my lap, he laughs. "Vik likes anal, kiddo. You into having a big, Russian cock up your door number two?"

I cringe at this, so crass. Trixie just laughs and says, "Everything for a price."

"Oh wait," Tyler says, eyes bleary with drink, a wide grin on his young face, "I forgot. He likes to lick assholes. Bend over and let him lick your asshole."

The other guys hoot and holler, and Trixie, spurred by the attention, turns and says, "I'll do you one better."

"Get out your cameras, gentlemen," Tyler announces, pulling his phone from his pocket.

Trixie goes to the bar and grabs a cherry. She pulls down her thong, exposing her ass to everyone in the room. For a sick, short moment, I consider throwing her onto the card table for a hard fuck. I have been thinking about Scarlett incessantly since I arrived. I feel wired with sexual energy and need to release some of it—badly.

My attention turns back to the stripper, who has now put the stem of the cherry in the crack of her arm bent at the elbow to look like it is up her asshole. The little red fruit hangs out as she invites me to get it out with my mouth.

"What the hell," I mumble to myself.

"Not the weirdest thing I've seen in a strip joint," Georg comments.

I lean in as Trixie says, "Give it a good lick, stud."

I feel very buzzed. In the back of my mind, I feel this is a bad idea, but I push it down, and shove my tongue into the crack of Trixie's arm, who yelps as I swirl my tongue around before grabbing the cherry with my teeth.

The guys all erupt in cheers as I chew up the sweet cherry. Trixie pulls her G-string back up and turns, red-cheeked. She leans in and says, "I'd give anything to see what you can do to the real thing. Holy hell, you have a sexy tongue!"

"That's going on Snapchat, yo!" Tyler hoots.

"Wait. What is this snap chat?"

"Oh, I forgot you don't do social media." He pulls up something on his phone and shows me. "I post it, but it goes away after a certain amount of time. No evidence later."

"I do not like this," I say, feeling my face scrunch into some mixture of confusion and concern.

"Don't worry," he says, slapping me on the back. "It'll be gone by morning, but it's just too good to keep from the world."

I hear Evan say, "Holly will have a fucking stroke if she sees it."

"We're off-season. She should be off-season, too," Tyler says, pouting.

"She never takes a break," he says. "It's never off-season to Holly Laurent-Kazmeirowicz."

Georg snorts at this. "Well, I think I might try that cherry trick on Pam later."

Tyler comes up with an idea for a game. He gets several straight-back chairs brought in, and rope. He has me, Georg, and Mikhail each sit in one, and he takes the fourth. We have our hands and feet tied to the chair and the women are supposed to straddle and ride us as hard as they can. The first to get a chair to tip over is the winner and gets a big tip.

This seems like a stupid game to me, but Evan agrees to film it and referee. I go along, lost in the haze of drink. We are all fully-clothed, so there is no real humping, but the action does feel good. Trixie is too small to make me fall over, though, and it is the dark-haired girl who wins, knocking Georg to his back after some wild and raucous movements.

He hits the ground and yelps, "Ouch!" before

cracking up. I have to admit this is a pretty amusing scene.

"Funny," I hear myself say, my lips curling into something of a smirk.

"Hey—that's almost an emotion out of Demoskev!" Mikhail yells.

"Fuck yeah!" Tyler yelps. "Let's do it again!"

We play this stupid game for a while longer before finally stumbling out into the night, left to figure out our ways back to the hotel.

17
dirty dog!!!

Scarlett

I wake up with a start. I swear I heard…

Where am I, exactly?

I look around and see a pair of feet. I've fallen asleep on the couch in Pam's suite. Devon's freshly pedicured feet are in my face as I sit up, and I see Daisy asleep in a chair. There are empty wine bottles and glasses strewn around amongst snack bags, empty plates, and a half-eaten pizza.

We had a pretty good night, I guess.

The sounds that woke me up start again and I look around, realizing Holly and Evan are out on the balcony, seemingly having an argument.

The sliding door is slightly open, letting their voices in.

"What the hell were you thinking, Evan?" Holly wails. "Screwing around with nasty strippers?"

"We were just having a bit of fun, baby. Nothing happened."

"There is shit all over social media," she snaps. "All over. Tyler must have posted fifteen videos to Snap. And there are still images all over every other platform because people screen-shotted stuff. Oh my God, I can't believe this."

"It was funny," Evan yells, but not in a mean way. In fact, he seems very calm, almost amused by her level of wrath this early in the morning.

"Did you screw someone else last night?" She breaks into tears.

Evan lets out a chuckle and pulls her into a hug. He kisses her head, but she pushes him away. "Don't just laugh at me. Tell me the truth!"

Pam comes out of the bedroom, tying the belt of a silk robe around her waist before sliding the door farther open and stepping out into the bright, morning sun.

"Hey, you're waking up the whole suite," she says calmly. "What's going on?"

"Did you see everything on social media this morning?" Holly asks.

"No. It's, like, seven in the morning. I haven't even looked at my phone yet."

Holly shoves her phone in Pam's face. "Look. Those guys were all up in these strippers' business last night."

"Babe, you're overreacting," Evan says calmly.

"Don't tell me I'm overreacting," Holly explodes. "I have to manage these messes. This stuff affects my work. Plus, you're married to me! You're only supposed to want me!"

She starts crying again; her face red and wet with tears. Evan pulls her to him again, wrapping her up into his big body. "Holly, babe, I love you. I *don't* want anyone else. I would never sleep with someone else. We were just having a bit of fun."

"Holly," Pam says as she flips through the images on Holly's phone, "I have to agree with Evan. It all looks like good fun to me. It was Georg's bachelor party. They all got wasted and had some tits flashed in their faces. No big deal."

"What about that video of Viktor? He had his tongue up some stripper's ass," Holly yells back.

"That's Viktor." Pam calmly explains, "Viktor is single. Not married. He can stick his tongue wherever he wants. The worst I see here is some dumb game where Georg got knocked on his head."

"Plus," Evan explains, "that video of Viktor isn't what you're thinking it is…"

"I saw it. He ate a cherry from a stripper's ass."

"Not her arse. It was the fold of her arm making a crease above her elbow. It just looked like her arse. One of Tyler's absurd pranks. Viktor was pissing drunk, yes, but even he knew where that cherry was…and it definitely wasn't in her arsehole!" I've never seen Evan so defensive before, his slight British accent coming through loud and clear.

Whatever," Holly says, fuming. "I'm going home. To our baby. This is embarrassing."

Storming back into the suite, Holly grabs her bags before stomping out and letting the door slam behind her. I'm still a little bleary from the bottle-and-a-half of wine I put down on my own last night. The sound of the slamming door hurts my head.

Pam puts a hand on Evan to hold him back from running after her. They talk quietly, but I can still hear them.

"I think she's hormonal," Pam says.

"Maybe." Evan sighs and runs his hands through his hair.

"Dude, when is the last time she had her period?"

Evan thinks on this for a second, then his eyes go wide. "Oh my God. You don't think?"

Pam shrugs and makes a face. "Well, is it possible?"

"I mean, yeah…it's bloody possible…"

Evan gives Pam a quick hug and runs for the door. I mean *runs*. He sprints out, yelling Holly's name, hoping to catch her before she leaves.

I try not to let Pam see that I've witnessed this whole exchange, forcing my eyes shut as a million thoughts run through my head. First, I guess I've been unfair to Holly. Things are never perfect for anyone, and she and Evan are obviously having a hard time. This weekend has given me my first glimpse of female friendship in a very long time and I'm sympathetic to Holly, who takes her job so seriously that she lets it seep into her personal life.

I grab my phone from the coffee table and open up Snapchat, trying to figure out what the big deal is. Some of the videos make me giggle. They are truly stupid, and while there's definitely some stripper action happening, there's nothing more than just a bunch of drunk dummies having a good time. Well, except for the aforementioned video of Viktor. It really does look like he licks a stripper's ass crack. And eats a cherry out of it. There's no way to tell it's really her arm like Evan said. It could be her ass.

It makes me wonder if he gets it on more than I thought. Who knows what else he did off-screen? Maybe he took that red-haired stripper back to his room. Maybe he did the same things to her that he did to me. Maybe he did more? The doubt returns. He never texted me back last night and after seeing this video of him, I certainly know why. He's probably moved on. I was too crazy, asked too many questions. I let my baggage get in the way of what could have been a good, healthy, Netflix-and-chill relationship.

And he's probably not trustworthy for more than that anyway.

I end up heading up to my own suite to shower. I take a long nap and call in sick for my shift at Tangiers. I never hear from Viktor, which solidifies my assumption. He went home with the stripper. I curse myself. I like him too much and yet I barely know him. I let myself care too much about what he's doing. I shouldn't have yelled at him. Shouldn't have asked so many questions.

I never should have slept with him in the first place.

My head is all over the place. I don't eat all day and by the time I need to get ready for the rehearsal dinner, I'm in a really crappy mood.

I pull on my little black dress, the one I felt was too immature for this crowd and pull my hair back into its messy bun. I keep my makeup light with a little eyeliner and mascara and light pink lip gloss, and then pull on a pair of sky-high red, patent-leather heels.

At dinner, I sit far away from Viktor, purposely not looking at him. I flirt openly with Tyler, who is only too happy to flirt right back. It's all harmless, but I can see Viktor's lips are set in a deep frown. Deeper than usual, and I think, *"Good, serves you right, dickhead."*

I get a text during dessert.

Viktor: I got texts. Left phone in room. Did not get until this morning.

Scarlett: No worries. Those were a mistake.

I look up and see him staring at me, his gaze intense. He looks back down quickly and types something else on his phone. Immediately, Tyler's phone buzzes and he looks down at it, letting out a hearty laugh in response.

"Big guy's got his panties in a twist. Told me he'd crush my balls if I didn't stay away from you," he says, still laughing. "Fucking weirdo."

"You love him," I say. "You two have some sort of bromance or something. It's like Evan and Georg two-point-oh."

He snorts at this. "It's hard to be friends with a rock."

We both giggle and clink our glasses together. He's right. It is hard to be friends with a rock. Hard to have a relationship with a rock, too.

Except...that rock seems jealous. Which is kind of good, maybe...right? *But why? He did who knows what with a stripper last night.* Move. On. Woods.

> Viktor: You look beautiful tonight.
>
> Viktor: You are glowing. I want to kiss your neck. Badly.

Doh!

Nope. He doesn't just get to melt me with sexy words. No, sir.

> Scarlett: Not working.
>
> Viktor: The flush on your chest says otherwise.
>
> Scarlett: It's just the lighting. Not flushing.
>
> Viktor: I would bet your sweet cunt is dripping right now.
>
> Viktor: I want to lap it up. Suck on your clit.

> Scarlett: What is up with you tonight? Dirty Dog!!!

> Viktor: Red Rocket

> Viktor: I think of you always. I thought of you with my cock in my hand last night.

> Scarlett: You mean with your cock buried in a redhead's ass?

> Scarlett: Yeah, I saw that video.

> Viktor: We should talk.

I look up and I can feel that my cheeks are heated. My whole body is overheating. I'm so upset with him. Confused by him. I don't even know what I want from him. But I know his words are turning me on. But I'm also hurt. One rebuttal from me and he slept with someone else. *Surely three strikes and he's out, Scarlett?*

Just as I start to type that, Evan taps his glass with his fork and stands. Everyone's attention turns to him, where he reaches out and pulls Holly to her feet. She's cute tonight, wearing a light pink dress, her hair in a long, side ponytail that falls down past her chest. She looks like the goddess she is, and Evan looks at her that way. There is such love on his face that it nearly steals the breath from my lungs. Whatever was bothering them earlier has been worked out, and then some.

"I know this whole week is all about my good friend Georg, and Holly's best friend, Pam. And I couldn't be happier that these two crazy kids found each other. They are a perfect fit. But I also want to tell you all first…Holly is pregnant."

There are a lot of surprised noises around the table. Their baby, Danya, isn't even yet a year old. I have to guess that this second baby wasn't planned. Wasn't expected.

Still, he seems so happy. He's beaming, nearly in joyful tears as he pulls her to him, kissing her deeply.

"Geesh, get a room, Kazmeirowicz," someone yells.

"Well, shit, at least he can't get her pregnant," someone else responds, to resulting laughter around the table.

Pam and Georg get up and give them both hugs. I hear Pam say, "I friggin' knew it."

"Knew what?" Holly asks.

"Knew you had a bun in the oven," Pam answers. "You're so controlled most of the time, but you've been a total roller coaster lately."

Holly just grunts in response, rolling her eyes. She looks at Evan, who winks and kisses her again. I see her nipples harden beneath the sheer fabric of her dress and I can't help but think that if a person could get pregnant twice at the same time, tonight might be the night.

Viktor stares at me through this whole, crazy

scene. I feel his eyes on me, more than see them. And it makes my nipples pearl, as well. I want him. I can't lie about that. It's the only thing I'm sure of right now.

We don't talk, though. We go through the rehearsal and one more painful flash-mob practice, and then I leave.

I go up to my room and shut off my phone.

I go to sleep.

And I dream.

In Russian.

THE WEDDING IS in just a few hours. Georg and Pam are heading to their destination honeymoon on a private island off the Carolina coast this evening. Georg's whole family will be joining them in a week or so all the way from Russia since they couldn't get here in time for the Vegas nuptials. They will have a second beachside ceremony for their families to witness on the island, which is wonderful. I'm very happy for my friends.

I get up and shower, then cruise the shops to find something appropriate to wear. I find a cute maxi dress that is almost the same color as my hair. It's probably too casual, with its deep V neckline and empire waist, but it's pretty and I think I can dress it up with accessories.

I dress quickly, adding chunky, gold jewelry and gold sandals. I do dramatic, gold eye makeup that really highlights my green eyes. I leave my hair long and loose and a little wild.

The effect works. Viktor practically salivates when he sees me, his eyes slowly working the length of me as I stand, watching the short, sweet, and funny marriage of Pam and Georg. I try to focus on the couple. They are so perfect for each other, matching each other's witty comments, both light and happy and clearly deeply in love. When they kiss, it heats up the room.

Holly, her maid of honor, cries through the whole ceremony. Evan, on the other side, grins at her, visibly still on cloud nine from the news of baby number two. Holly's uncle Troy holds baby Danya in the audience. He's a good-looking man, with hair that's flecked with gray. I'm distracted by Viktor only long enough to wonder why Troy never married, banking the question for a later conversation with Holly.

At the reception, I spend time talking with some of my other colleagues, keeping a careful distance from Viktor. He looks incredibly handsome in a tailored, gray suit. He wears a white shirt, open at the top button, no tie. It's a sexy look that he wears very well. A little too dangerously well for my self-control. And I want to lick that bit of exposed skin at his throat. So, sue me.

I. Cannot. Help. It.

Our flash mob goes really well. The guests love it, and of course, Holly is on her phone posting it to the team's social media feeds. The woman literally never stops working.

When we send off the newlyweds, I feel emotional, hugging Pam tightly. I can only contribute my melancholy to this being the first wedding I've attended since Stephen died. *By now, I should have had my own special wedding day. Been the beautiful bride.* But that was stolen from me...Yet, I did gain a new direction and new friends, and I cannot begrudge that.

"Thank you for being my friend," I say as we embrace. "I love you."

"Awww, Scarlett, you're going to make me cry." Pam kisses me on the cheek.

"It's been such a long time since I've had real girlfriends and I'm just so very happy I got to know you."

"I'm not moving away," she says, playfully nudging me. "Just going on my honeymoon. I'll call you as soon as we get back."

"Go, go," I say, wiping a tear from my cheek. "You're beautiful. He's beautiful. You'll make beautiful babies."

"Oh, God, I hope not," she exclaims. "At least not yet. I've only just got Georg out of diapers."

We both giggle and he rolls his eyes, leaning in for a quick hug.

"That big asshole really likes you," Georg says. "Make him behave."

They move along and I catch Viktor's gaze, once more feeling that stupid, crazy spark of want that buzzes between us like electricity.

As soon as our friends leave, I book it. I have one more night in the hotel suite and I intend to soak away all thoughts of Viktor in the huge tub. I strip off my clothes, run the hot water, and dump in a bunch of bubble bath. I pull my hair up on top of my head and sink into the water with an audible sigh of satisfaction.

As I soak, I think of this week. Of the women I've hung out with, of the laughs we've shared. I know it sounds cheesy, but I miss it already. I miss these women and these new friendships I've built.

I know I've not let people in these past couple of years. During my time with Stephen, I was overwhelmed. I was focused on him, on his increasing issues. I worked and I went home, or I went out to find him. Stressful is an understatement. And when he died...I just shut down. I shut people out, including my father, who went missing shortly after Stephen's suicide. The two most important people in my life were gone, and I was alone with debt up to my eyeballs, no education, and no way of ever saving enough to be free of Las Vegas and all its heartbreaking memories.

I'm lost deep in thought when a loud knock sounds at the door. I jump up, pulling a thin, silk robe over my wet body and shuffling quickly to the door wondering if it's one of the girls up for one last night of decadence in this awesome suite.

But when I open it, Viktor is there, still in his suit.

He steps inside and lets the door shut, his eyes meeting mine.

"I need to talk to you." *God, that deep voice of his...*

The sound is delicious and I'm suddenly ultra-aware that I am nearly naked, but for this wet and totally see-through silk robe. My breasts hang heavily, aching, and my nipples are pebbled, ready for his touch.

But I must stand firm. There are a lot of questions about Viktor Demoskev that need some answers.

"What do you want to talk about?"

"Us. This thing that is between us."

"There is no us. We had sex. That's all," I say, my chin jutting out defiantly.

"Your body says otherwise. It always gives you away."

"So I'm turned on by you," I say dismissively. "So what? You already know you can make me come. It doesn't mean I want to marry you."

"No, perhaps not," he says, stepping closer. "You are correct. There is more than sex between us. What it is, I do not know for sure."

"It's just lust." My words sound ridiculously weak.

"What is it you want from me, Scarlett?"

"I don't want..." I breathe in and out quickly. "I

don't think you're being honest about who you really are. I don't feel like I can trust you."

"There is no reason not to trust," he says with a shake of his head. "I have done nothing of concern."

"You make bets on sports. You hang with creepy guys with creepy briefcases. Are you in the mafia?" I blurt all of this out. It's word-vomit soup.

He lets out a humorless chuckle. "This again. Is nothing."

"Is nothing," I repeat in a bad imitation of his accent. "Okay, well then what did you do with that stripper after you licked her butthole and ate a cherry out of it?"

"Was not her butthole." He shakes his head and looks uncomfortably guilty.

I scoff at this. "I told you already that I watched the video."

"No. Was her elbow. Truly. No excuse for licking. I was drunk, but I did not do more. I thought of you all night. I came in my own hand thinking of you."

Oh.

Well, there's that again.

The thought of strong, masculine, muscly Viktor with his huge cock in his hand really, really turns me on. Like, a lot. I lose my train of thought just picturing it.

It must be obvious, because Viktor steps even closer, his knuckles grazing against my sensitive breasts, outside of the thin, wet fabric.

I lean into him. It's an unconscious thing,

uncontrollable. My body recognizes this, wants this. I'm getting wetter from just this tiny touch.

Viktor leans down, his lips grazing my neck, his tongue darting out to taste my skin. I sigh as his hand lifts the short hem of my robe, his fingers dipping between my legs for some quick strokes. He pulls away just as quickly, leaving me breathless, wanting so much more.

He licks his fingers slowly, his eyes never leaving mine.

"I do not lie, Scarlett. I hate dishonesty. I am not mafia. I do bet on some MMA tournaments, but it's not frequent. Not necessary."

I dip my head as I don't want to look into his hazel eyes and see dishonesty. *More lies.* But then I consider our interactions to date. He hasn't shirked from stating facts, just not seen the necessity to clarify. *I don't think he's a liar.* I'm still wary, but I do know what deceit looks like.

He reaches up and puts his fingers under my chin, lifting it. "Let me take you away. Scarlett...My Red Rocket. Pack a bag and let me take you away from here. We will talk. Get to know each other. Maybe find pleasure again and again."

"I have this suite for another..." I start the sentence and then realize it's stupid to finish it. I *want* to go with Viktor. Very much.

So, I just nod and ask him for a few minutes to change and throw an overnight bag together. He says he'll be waiting for me in the lobby. I watch him leave; the door shutting behind him, and try to gather myself. I'm incredibly turned on. Aching. I can't believe I let him out of this room without taking him to bed.

But now I'm turning in my chips.

Because I've given up resisting him.

Wherever we go next, I'm his.

For as long as it lasts.

18
possible b.s.

Viktor

Lake Tahoe, Nevada

With the help of a computer voice on my cell phone, I drive us to Lake Tahoe from the airport at Reno. Honestly, I had no plan when I showed up at Scarlett's room. I wanted to strip her naked and take her right then and there. Her wet, flimsy robe had me straining to keep my cock contained.

How is it I could go so many months without sex and now I can think of nothing but? It is her, but why? I don't know a single thing about her. Not really. Only that she is beautiful and sensual. Our bodies fit together like they were made for one another. How can I want someone so badly that I know so little?

I asked the concierge at the LINQ for ideas and he

suggested booking a cabin retreat at the lake, the flight only a little over an hour from Las Vegas to Reno. He also arranged a rental car to be waiting for us when we landed. I tipped him handsomely to manage the details for me, and as we near the check-in office, I feel I could have tipped him even more.

The sky is bright blue, disappearing under a canopy of evergreen trees as we pull down a long drive. I have Scarlett wait as I check us in, and then drive us farther into the site, until we reach a quaint cottage along the water. We drop our bags and walk to the back door, taking in the view of the lake from a small, private deck. There are no other cottages in our immediate view, but we can see white-capped mountains in the distance.

"I've never been to Lake Tahoe before," she says, a little breathlessly. "Can you believe it? It's so close and I've never been here."

"Have you ever left Las Vegas, Scarlett?"

She blushes, a rarity, and shakes her head. "I'm embarrassed to admit it, but, no. Not really."

I tilt my head and consider this. "Why does this embarrass you?"

She shrugs. "You're just...you've seen the whole world. I haven't been anywhere."

"Well, now you have been here. What a beautiful place to start."

She gives me a small, grateful smile and returns inside.

"There are bicycles. Though I am very big and will look stupid on one."

Again, a tiny smile. "Should we go for a swim? Or take a hike? What do we do first?" Her questions are punctuated by the sound of her stomach rumbling loudly.

"Well, I think that the first is to get food. I will go find us something."

"I guess I am hungry. I didn't eat much at the wedding."

"And it is dinner time. I apologize for not thinking of this in our plans. I will come back with pizza. Is that okay?"

"Pizza is great, Viktor. Thank you."

I don't actually know where to get pizza, but I have to meet Oleg and Vasily for another piss test. It is a cumbersome, tiresome practice, but the Russian officials require testing windows every twenty-four to thirty-six hours for a week straight each month. It is a practice meant to prove, beyond a shadow of a doubt, that all captures are clean and consistent.

We meet near the check-in cottage, and I piss quickly in the restroom, Vasily there to watch as always. They also agree to take two bets to the bookies for an MMA fight this evening. As I hand them a wad of cash to handle the bet, I see her. Scarlett has followed me on a bicycle.

I speak in Russian, telling the guys to get moving, then head in to ask about having food delivered to the cottage. The manager says he can have pizza and drinks sent to us.

When I walk back out, Scarlett stands in front of the door, hands tightly crossed against her breasts. "What was all that? Why were those guys here? What the hell is going on?" She is being crazy again. This is not how I wanted things to go for us.

"Let us talk about this at the cottage please."

"No," she says firmly. "I want answers now."

"I *said*, we will talk at the cottage. Get in the car."

"Don't tell me what to do," she shouts, that fiery red-headed temper flaring. "What kind of corrupt gambling ring are you involved in? And what do they have on you? How much do you owe?"

I don't know where this is coming from, but I need to talk to her in private. People are starting to stare. I grab her arm and drag her to the car. "Get in," I order. There is no argument to be broached as I open the door. She gets in and I shut it, grabbing the bike, and tossing it into the back of the SUV.

It is not until we are back in the cottage that I speak.

"You must stop talking about this, Scarlett. Gambling. Mafia. Corruption. It is not like that. This thing I must do. I piss."

"You...piss?" She is clearly confused.

"I piss in a cup to prove I am not on performance-enhancing drugs," I explain. "It is something my Russian agents require as backup to American tests, and it also creates a record for

Olympic players. It is annoying, but it allows proof that I am clean."

"The briefcases?" she asks, somewhat stunned.

"Medical testing supplies. Latex gloves. Piss cups. Plastic bags. Vasily and Oleg both work for my agent."

"But you do...gamble. On sports. I saw you hand them money to bet on a fight."

"Yes, I bet in off-season. Never on hockey and never during the sports season. I place bets on MMA. It is a hobby of mine, fighting. I enjoy it."

"You do mixed martial arts?" Her voice is now small. Her temper abated.

"I do. This is why I wished to spend time here. To have you know more about me. To learn more about you."

"Oh." Her answer is so simple. I don't know how to take it.

"I have our dinner ordered," I say, filling the silence. "I do not know how long it will take. Perhaps an hour. Would you like to take bicycle ride as we talk?"

She nods. "Sure."

As expected, I look comical on a bicycle, as evidenced by Scarlett's smirk. She looks lovely on an old-fashioned, yellow bike with a basket in front. It has a small bell, which she rings, grinning widely.

"I would take a photograph of you like this," I say. I can't figure out how to say that the light hits her hair in just a certain way. She looks youthful and sweet on this silly bicycle. Not like me, so big and clunky on a blue machine that is far too small for me. She laughs at me fumbling with my phone as I take several photos. She even poses under a tree for me when I ask her to.

We ride along a marked path and Scarlett is the first to talk.

"I was engaged once," she begins. "His name was Stephen. He was a world-class poker player and an addict. A gambling addiction led to a drug addiction. And when he started losing, his life fell apart. He lost everything and then I lost him. I got roughed up by some Russian mafia thugs he owed money to, and he killed himself."

Ublyudok. The bastard. Coward.

And I barely keep hold of my anger as Scarlett tells me very graphic details about her assault, about her relationship with her fiancé, and about the money she still fears she owes them. No wonder she was terrified of Oleg and Vasily, thinking they were mafia. And to think her father also left her with his debts. How would she ever want to trust another man?

"I am sorry, Scarlett. To know you have had to endure such tragedy...for someone so young."

She waves me off as we ride. "I'm done feeling sorry for myself. It's just that I can't be with another addict. Do you hear what I'm saying?"

"But I am no addict," I say clearly. "Is hobby."

"I want to believe you, Viktor, I do. But I don't

know anything about you. You're not exactly the sharing type. You know what I mean?"

"Well, this is first we have had time to talk," I argue.

"I guess that's fair. So now I know you grew up in Saint Petersburg, you played in the Olympics, and you like to do MMA. What else?"

"Do you ever think your fiancé's death was not suicide?" I have the beginning of working a theory in my mind. "Perhaps it was murder?"

"I've thought of that." She stops her bike abruptly on the trail in front of me. "We should probably turn back. To meet the delivery guy, remember?"

"Probably yes," I agree. We turn our bikes around and take the trail back to the cottage.

"I tried to push the possibility of murder with the police, but beyond my own assault, there was no sign of violence. It looked like straight suicide. I was told by the medical examiner that he just took one too many pills for his body to handle."

I find this very suspicious, but do not press her further. "Your father was also in debt? To Russians?"

"Yes...he may be dead, too, for all I know."

"You have not looked for him?"

"I didn't have the money and I had no idea where to start my search." She sounds sad and I understand why. So many unhappy experiences in her young life.

I have an idea, but I don't share it with her. Not yet.

"Do you have hobbies?" I change the subject.

"Not so much anymore. I used to think I was going to be on a big dance squad because I danced all through high school. But I started working full time right after graduation and then I got with Stephen and…"

She sighs and the meaning is implied. She gave up whatever dreams she once had. She works to survive, now. Scarlett is so much more than just the red-headed beauty I met a week ago. She's a fighter. A survivor. And I know all about those. She asked about my love of MMA. Does she have similar outlets?

"You must do some things for just fun?" I insist.

"I go out sometimes. More lately, now that I've made some friends at work. But I work full time for the Crush, and then the extra hours at the Tangiers… doesn't leave much time for anything else. This week has been like a vacation, really, with the office closed. It's been a new experience for me having so many free days."

"You like your job doing press for the Crush?"

"I do." Her beautiful face breaks into a smile that lights up the room. "It's been fun for the most part. A little boring at times. I liked doing Holly's job while she was on maternity leave. I could do that for a living, for sure, but I still have a lot to learn."

"Perhaps you will have more chances now that Holly is having second child."

"Mmm," she hums. "I doubt it. Holly is a rock star. She's not going anywhere."

Once we return to the cottage, we store our

bicycles and head inside. Scarlett disappears to the bathroom while I greet the pizza delivery man, who has brought not just pizza but also a six-pack of beer. When Scarlett returns, she asks if I would like to eat outside on the patio. She has found a red and black picnic blanket in a cupboard and lays it on the table.

As we eat, we talk more about her fiancé and the abuse she incurred at the hands of his bookies. How the fuck had that man been so blind with his addictions that he lost track of the safety of the woman he supposedly loved? I know Galina's husband, Heinrich, would protect her with his life. Gambling debts must always be paid—with money or blood. I cannot imagine why they stopped contacting her. Why? With her fiancé dead...Scarlett lives in fear that they will come for this money, but they have not after two years. *Yet.* Something is not right in this scenario.

Makes sense why she has never been outside this city. She is a small-town girl in some ways, exposed to the world through the caricatures she has seen throughout Las Vegas. I suddenly feel strongly to show her the world, to take her far away so that she can breathe fresh air, air that is not tainted by the mistakes of the men in her life.

"Have you ever been in a relationship?" She asks the question casually as we sip our beer, watching the sun set over the lake.

"Once. She was a dancer."

"Was?"

"Well, likely is still, but I have not considered her for a long time."

"Why did you end things?" she asks after a moment of silence watching the sunset.

"Is hard to be with someone who is as committed to sport as you are." I give her a dismissive shrug. "My goal is to play hockey. The relationship created a detour from that goal."

"That's sad," she says, giving me a pitying look. "You're so married to hockey that you couldn't figure out how to make a relationship work?"

"But I did not end it."

"Oh...I'm sorry for assuming otherwise. And?"

"And I decided that the hurt was not worth it. I doubled my focus on hockey. That is all."

"Nothing since?"

"No," I answer, taking a long pull from my beer bottle. "Sex and relationships are not priorities for me."

There is another moment of silence, so I look over at Scarlett, who is staring off in the other direction, her jaw set. I realize my mistake.

"I am sorry. I do not mean to make less of our time together. I mean only that I have not been interested in such things for a long time. Until I saw you. True."

"That's just a line of BS you're feeding me."

"BS?"

"Bullshit," she snaps. "That just does not happen, Viktor. Men don't swear off sex and relationships and then, like, boom, they're suddenly all up and into someone. I swear I think you live a double life. Or you're hiding how sexually active you really are. I mean, I've been sexually active. I can admit it. People like having sex. There's nothing wrong with that."

"Scarlett…"

"Viktor," she shoots back.

I sigh. "I liked having sex with you. Very much. I have thought of nothing else since."

"Really?"

I nod. "Really. And I did feel this…boom…that you speak of. I noticed you, in the locker room. Many other women try to get my attention, but it was you I noticed. Only you."

"But…why?" Her voice has turned to a whisper.

"Why is anything? At first, purely physical. Your red hair. Your curvy body. The sound of your voice. It was appealing to me."

"And then?"

"And then," I say, standing and walking the few steps to position myself in front of where she sits on top of the table. "And then, perhaps, a game? You pushed me away. You told me no, and I was wanting to win you. At least for one night."

Our eyes meet and I see longing there. Emotional and physical. I am not so adept at reading women—I have little experience, really—but I see what she needs. She needs to hear good things, nice things. She needs to know this has moved past one night.

"Well," she says, clearing her throat, "that one night was pretty spectacular. At least...it was for me."

"For me as well. I told you, I have not stopped thinking of you. Of the way our bodies fit. I feel like an animal with this constant wanting. What have you done to me?"

"I feel the same but...is this—" She stops and swallows. Takes a breath. "Is it...just sex?"

"Is it for you?" I stare into her eyes as I ask the question. Maybe I can read her body language for a better understanding of her.

"I don't know?" Her answer is a question. She frowns slightly. It is very endearing.

"We do not have to figure it out now. Or tomorrow. It can be what it will be. Yes?"

Scarlett bites her lower lip and I lean in, kissing it softly. She releases her lip and opens for me. My tongue explores her mouth, the roof, her teeth, her tongue. Probably without even knowing, she spreads her legs wider. I lean in closer, pushing her back on the soft blanket, pushing the empty pizza box out of the way.

We kiss with her lying on the table, a buffet ready for eating. And I do. I nibble at her ears and neck. I kiss her lips and her clavicle. I pull up her T-shirt and reveal those heavy breasts, contained in a silver lace bra. The color contrasts against her pale skin beautifully, but it is hiding what I need to see and kiss and suck right now. So I pull down on the cups of her bra and force those pretty nipples to pop out over the fabric. I lick and kiss and tease both with my teeth in alternating bites, some gentle and some harder. She arches toward me each time, soft moans escaping her lips.

When I see her shiver, I realize the night has descended, cooling the air outside. I put her lovely tits back into her bra and help her to sit up. After setting her down from the table onto her own two feet, I take her hand in mine to walk back inside the cottage. She leads us straight for the bedroom. Scarlett has a purpose. I am more than happy to watch the show of her stripping out of her clothes. Who am I to stifle her demonstration of getting naked for me? I am not fucking stupid.

Slowly, she lifts her shirt over her head before tossing it away with a sexy smirk. Then she unhooks her pretty silver bra from behind her back. She takes her time sliding the straps down over each shoulder in turn before letting gravity take it to the floor with a rustle.

Standing before me, breasts bared—which are the prettiest pair I have ever known—with her hair like red wine around her shoulders and down her back. She is simply perfect even though she still wears her black jeans and sandals—which need to disappear as quickly as possible. There is something so very innocent about her despite the obvious sensuality she is putting on display for me. I am bewitched by this beguiling woman in so many ways. Her beauty is something she does not even seem to be aware of.

"What?" She blushes shyly.

"You are perfect. A bewitching goddess."

She pushes her lips together, the flush of pink staining her cheeks.

I pull my shirt over my head as well and toss it away. She admires me as I strip down. I notice how her green eyes darken and her creamy skin flushes in anticipation. My cock is already hard, springing up with a bounce as I get rid of my pants and step forward to help Scarlett out of hers. I jerk the buttons free and push them down over her hips, exposing a tiny strip of matching silver lace to her bra. I can't help chuckling.

"What's so funny?"

I fall to my knees, still chuckling. "These can hardly be classified as panties."

She doesn't get a moment to respond before I shove my face between her legs, ready to worship her. I lick and suck at her through the thin lace, feeling her wetness, smelling her sweet arousal. Eventually, I push the tiny piece of fabric aside and shove my tongue into her, my hands grabbing her bare ass cheeks and pulling her forward.

I want her riding my face until she comes. My Red Rocket does not disappoint me either. With a heavy sigh and a deep moan escaping her lips, she buckles beneath my tongue devouring every part of her it can reach.

Her little moans turn me on. "I want you to come. And I want to hear you," I tell her as I tear away her thong. I need her completely naked so I can enjoy every bare inch of her.

"Give me this," I say as I pull her back to my mouth. With her cunt attached to my face I work over her clit with my tongue. When I push two of my fingers inside her she curses, dirty words that only serve to fuel my desire for more.

"Yes, yes," she chants. "Yes. Yes. Fuck. Fuck, that feels so good. God, I'm so close. Fuck."

Her whole pussy clenches and her body stops moving. The pulsating of her clit is palpable against my tongue. It lasts and lasts, and then she goes nearly boneless, falling back against the bed.

I stand and look at my handiwork. Her swollen pussy lips and clit, the wetness that streaks her inner thighs. Her flushed, rosy cheeks and breasts. And I realize that this will never be enough. I don't know what it is about her. There are so many things to learn. And she may not like me very much if we continue down this path. But I want to try.

I lean in with care, kissing her gently as she recuperates from her explosive orgasm. She responds, her arms snaking around my back to pull me down onto the bed with her.

"So good," she says quietly. "This is so good with you."

I could not agree more with her.

I slip inside her quietly, without preamble, loving the feel of her tight warmth around my aching cock.

"Yesss," I hiss. "You feel so fucking good."

I move slowly, at first, savoring each movement, each thrust, each corresponding kiss. But she is having none of it. No, she wants more, and harder, and faster. So, the pace quickens as I plunge in and out of her, our kisses getting rougher, sloppier.

She cries out as she comes again, her body going rigid as she clenches around my shaft. I keep fucking into her, the added friction pushing me to the edge.

"Come on me," she says breathlessly. "I want to see your cock in your hand coming all over me."

This is all I need. I pull out of her, stroking myself as she watches with heavy eyelids, her fingers playing at her clit. It is the sexiest thing I have ever seen, made all the sexier as I climax all over her fucking gorgeous tits and throat.

I fall beside her, breathing heavily. She runs a finger through a stream of cum and puts it to her mouth, tasting. I lean in and kiss her, our scents and tastes mingling. This just makes me want her again, and she seems keen, grabbing my cock in her hand and stroking it. My fingers find her soaked cunt again, and we prime each other through more kisses. Kissing...always kissing. I need her kisses. So many kisses...

When I am ready to go again, she pushes me to my back and mounts me, grinding over my cock with her back arched and her hair slapping against my balls and thighs as she moves up and down. I sit up slightly, pulling her closer, sucking her breasts, grazing her nipples with my teeth.

"Mmmm," she hums. "Yes. Yes. Do that. Yes, Viktor." I have discovered that Red Rocket likes a little pain along with her pleasure.

Her movements get faster and her eyes close as that now-familiar pulse begins inside of her. It just never stops. Minutes. Hours. I don't know. It could be days. She rides me, pumping against me, coming all over me. She's so wet.

When I come, it's nearly a surprise, a sharp spurt of intense pleasure, before I pick her up and carry her into the bathroom. The shower is small. Too small, really, but I turn on the faucet while still holding her against me, my cock still buried inside of her as I go back to kissing her soft, sweet lips. The water pummels us, hot and steaming, after we step inside, still kissing. Still fucking. I harden again, inside of her, and we just...keep going.

It's like a haze of drug, fucking Scarlett. I've never felt something so good in all my life.

I never want it to end.

19
star crossed lovers

Scarlett

It's very early in the morning. Monday, I think? I'm not even sure, to be honest. I need to get back to Vegas though before I lose one or both of my jobs.

Viktor is sleepy but awake, my head on his chest as he strokes my hair idly.

"I feel like we went to another planet last night," I comment with a yawn.

"It was out of this world, yes." His beard stubble rasps against my skin as he nuzzles my neck with a kiss. He has a fixation with my neck, I think. Lots and lots of kisses there from him.

I think about what he just said. A pun? From Viktor? I look up and find him smiling.

Like, a real smile, not just a smirk. It's very attractive. He has really nice teeth, which is a rarity among hockey players. Maybe a few are implants, but I like that he fixed his teeth rather than leave gaps like many guys do —waiting for their retirement from professional play before commencing with the dental repairs.

"You're smiling." The words come out sounding kind of dumbfounded and dazzled. Which I am.

"You make me happy, Red Rocket."

This takes my breath away. But still. "You shouldn't say things like that," I say softly, laying my head back on his chest.

"Why? Is true."

"It's just the glow of sexual satisfaction. It will wear off."

"That is true also, but I think there is more. A connection, as you have asked for. Yes?"

"Maybe." I roll to my back and stretch out like a cat. "But you have to leave for the summer. And staff isn't supposed to date team. We're doomed. Star-crossed lovers."

"Humph." His beautiful smile disappears as quickly as it appeared.

He stands and stretches, his arms over his head, showing off each glorious muscle in his back. His butt is phenomenal. Like, buns-of-steel good, and his legs are ridiculously defined.

"Do you enjoy this view?" he asks playfully.

"I do, yes. Thank you."

He turns, giving me the full monty of his front side. "And this?" The smile is back, but this time it's more of a wicked grin.

"Yep, that view's good, also. Especially that smile. When did you get so smiley?"

"More smiling only for you, each time we fuck like that."

Oof. He's so direct and literal. The things he says to me would be offensive coming from anyone else. But with Viktor? Off-the-freaking-chain hotness when it comes out of his mouth.

"You are kinda dirty, mister. The things you say are uber filthy."

"The things we do are uber filthy. You like filthy, I think."

"I might have liked it…" I give him my sexiest wink.

"You liked it four or five times last night."

"Ahh, it was more times than I could count."

"There is more we can do. More filthy than that."

"Oh, I'm sure there is." I let out a sigh. "But I really should get back to Vegas. I've got to work at the arena tomorrow. And I might already be fired from my other job."

"Okay, but I need to wish you a proper good morning first. I can do that in the shower…if you will join me." He holds out his hand to help me out of bed and gives me yet another magnificent smile. Viktor has no idea of the power *that* smile has over me. I fear I'll be putty in his hands whenever he lays one on me.

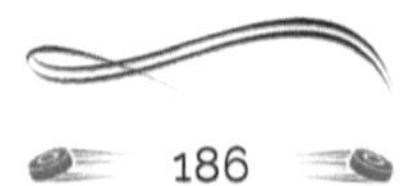

WHEN WE FINALLY HEAD OUT after some spectacular good-morning shower sex, I'm sad we have to leave our secluded little lake cabin behind.

"This was a perfect getaway, Viktor. Thank you for inviting me," I say as we walk to the car.

"You are most welcome, Red Rocket." He gives me a sweet kiss after buckling me into my seat first, then going around to get himself in. Always such a gentleman in his manners and behavior toward me. Viktor Demoskev was brought up to treat women with respect, that much is apparent. His refined manners off the ice are in complete contrast to the Mad Russian enforcer he becomes on the ice. Who would've guessed it? Not me. But I'm so glad I got the chance to find out at all.

We drive for a while in comfortable silence, just listening to the radio. A Demi Lovato song comes on. "Confident," it's called. I sing along, badly, and Viktor nods his head along. The boy really has zero rhythm.

"We're going to have to teach you to dance, big man," I joke.

"What do you mean? I am good dancer already."

"Slow dancing, yes. But anything with a beat? You are baaaad." I giggle. "Awful."

"That is offensive," he says, mock hurt. "You will have to make it up to me now."

"How could I possibly make up for the hurt I've caused by mocking your bad dancing?" I ask sweetly.

"Well, you can tell me why you say we are doomed. There is no reason to think such things."

"Oh, not what I thought you would ask for. Umm…I just think it will be hard to make this work. You're going to be gone. The team doesn't like fraternization. You know."

"That is…flimsy logic. You are grasping for reasons to sabotage this."

"This?" I laugh lightly even though I know what he means.

"This new thing between us. I told you, Scarlett, I have not been with a woman for a while. My focus has not been taken from hockey in a long time. I like you, and I like what we are together. Why should we not try?"

"Good sex notwithstanding, what else is there between us? Hot sexy times does not a long-term relationship make."

"There is time," he insists. "We can get to know each other more. We have only just begun. All things have a beginning."

"And an end," I argue. "And maybe it's best if we just enjoy this and let it go, so that we have good memories of it. It will never have a chance to fall apart if we end it now."

He growls—actually growls—and cracks his neck. "Scarlett, I know you are wary. Of me. Of who I am, or who you think I am. I know you have lost a love once before. I am not asking you to marry me. I am asking for us to give a try at this. Yes?"

"I don't know…"

"Think on it," he says confidently. "I must go to

Russia for summer league. I will do that phone call with the video with you. We will talk…and perhaps other filthy things."

"Phone sex, Viktor?" I raise an eyebrow.

"Yes, that. You will make yourself come for me while I watch you."

"So bossy."

"You like me bossy. And you will call."

Yes, sir.

20
better call saul

Two weeks later.

I'm trying not to be weepy about the fact that Viktor is off to Russia. I won't see him for at least eight more weeks, and as much as I put on the bravado and acted like things could never work between us, I really want them to.

I like him. And not just because he's hot and sexy and amazing in bed. That's an excellent bonus, of course, but mostly, I just feel really comfortable around him. Safe. Now that I know he's not in the mafia, not a gambling addict, and not throwing championship games for money, of course. I'm missing him terribly and it's only been a few short days since our memorable "goodbye" in a utility closet at the Tangiers.

Yeah, that one happened. Viktor surprised me at

work one night shortly after our return from our Lake Tahoe trip. He'd asked for my work schedule at Tangiers on the guise of planning time for us to be together as much as possible before he had to leave, but I found out real quick it was to watch over me while I was serving gamblers with wandering eyes—and to make sure they never evolved into wandering hands or anything even remotely resembling disrespect. Viktor is a very protective caveman it turns out. He would find somewhere to sit and hang out until I finished my shift. He'd order drinks and sometimes food, but he made it clear he was there for me. I can't stress enough how much that did to warm me to the idea of us having real relationship potential. He truly seems to understand my debatably irrational fears of being on some underworld hit list. He told me he only wants me to feel safe and to never have to worry about being assaulted or threatened for debts ever again. At the end of my shifts he'd be right there to follow me home or coax me over to his place to stay with him there. I did a few times, but we really didn't have that many opportunities to be together before he had to go away. We said our farewells the night before he was leaving for Moscow with a romantic dinner and dancing at the Bellagio. Followed up by a marathon of hot goodbye-sex in a suite that lasted well into the wee hours of the morning.

Obviously.

My body will be missing him just as much. And his dancing wasn't as terrible as I remember, either. To be fair, his slow-dancing moves are nothing to sneeze at. What he lacks in rhythm he more than makes up with his outstanding presentation. He's so pretty in his Euro-cut suit that I can't possibly notice much about his dance moves anyway. Especially when I'm in his arms while we're dancing. Hello—not made of stone here.

Viktor is far more cultured than most professional athletes I would guess. He's had more formal experiences in his life than your average NHL player. He's a romantic date. I've never been out with someone who pulled out all the stops with flowers and fancy hotel suites for wining, and dining, and dancing, and sexing, like Viktor-The Mad Russian-Demoskev does. Never would've thought he'd be that way in a million years. Preconceived impressions can be vastly different from the reality I have learned. It's best not to judge people until you have some experience with them and can really see how they conduct themselves. I remember Pam saying something like that about Georg. I wonder what she'll feel when I tell her about Viktor and me...when she finally gets home from her honeymoon.

I sigh dreamily thinking about the final night with Viktor. I'm supposed to be pulling together press releases on all of our post-season stories, but I've spent way more time pining over Viktor instead.

Fiona just ended our staff meeting for planning our summer coverage. As I trudge back to my desk, I wonder what he is up to all the way over in Moscow. Is he missing me as much as I am him? Does he have women busting down the doors to get his attention? Old girlfriends and hookups hoping to reconnect by sending him a "I heard you're back in town" text with a titty pic. I don't think Viktor would do that though. He asked me not to forget him over the summer, so I assume he won't be seeking out female companionship while he's away. But there's no way for me to really know that for sure. I barely know him at all.

I sigh and debate if I should start going to yoga class. It might help me channel my inner Zen, or at the very least, to locate the damn thing. That might be a good start, because I know I spend way too much time worrying about so many things as it is.

I see Holly go into Fiona's office and shut the door not long after our meeting is over. I noticed she was quiet during the staff meeting, which is very un-Holly-like. Usually she's got a million ideas, more than we can ever implement. She stays in there for a long time with the door closed…which basically gives me the green light to indulge in some more Viktor-daydreaming while I'm supposed to be working.

So, sue me. I can't seem to stop myself from doing it.

But that surprise extra last goodbye though…

I'd just finished serving a round and was on my way back to the bar with orders when my coworker, Nikki, sidled up to me with a sly wink. "You told me your big hockey stud was off to Russia for the summer."

"He is. His flight left this afternoon."

"Well, he didn't make his flight, honey, because he just asked me to cover you for a break. Tipped me very nicely too."

"What? Viktor's here?" I whip my head around and nearly dump my drink tray in the process.

"I told him to wait for you in the break room." She smiles knowingly. "You're welcome."

"Oh my God, Nikki, I love you." I give her my tray and kiss her on the cheek.

"Don't get caught, and I expect a detailed reporting, if you know what I mean," she calls after me, but I'm already booking it toward the break room.

I find him leaning against some Maker's Mark boxes stacked alongside the hallway, looking hot AF in black jeans and a long-sleeved cream shirt with every cut and curve of his muscles defined in glorious detail beneath the super-soft fabric. "What happened? Why are you still here in Vegas?"

"My flight changed to later one. I'm going to the airport now, but I told my driver to wait. I hoped to have one last goodbye with you."

"Oh, you beautiful man, come here." I hold out my arms to him and he meets me halfway, the two of us colliding in a powerful kiss that certainly needs

somewhere much more private than this employee backroom area.

"I was impulsive to come while you are working, I know, but I wanted to see you one more time before I go." He stops kissing me and holds my face in both of his hands, his eyes intense. "And to tell you I have arranged something for you while I am away."

"You arranged something...for me?"

"Just to ease your mind, and also for me to ease mine. I do not want you to be worrying about those thugs that hurt you before." He puts a shiny black business card into my hand. "You should call this guy if someone gives you trouble or follows you. His name is Saul Heisenberg. He is what's called a fixer and can take care of any problem. If you feel frightened or threatened, then you must call him. He will know who you are." Viktor kisses me gently on the lips in the sweetest way. Never could I have imagined Viktor Demoskev would be so caring and gentle and considerate. His big mean brute reputation is a facade apparently—not that I object in any way, but it's kind of shocking to fully accept that. "Will you do this for me, Scarlett? I want you feeling very safe even if I am not here to watch out for you. In this way I can still do it from afar."

I blink up at him in surprise, my eyes working rapidly to hold back the flood of tears that spring up uncontrollably. "Y-Yes, I so will. That's got to be the most generous thing anyone has ever done for me, Viktor. I can't believe you set that up for me." I am overcome with all kinds of emotions. I doubt even Viktor understands how much his gesture means. I certainly don't want to anticipate having to call this Saul guy, but simply knowing he's there to call is everything to me. "Thank you. You have no idea what this means…" I kiss him deeply, hoping to show him just how touched I am. But I pull my lips away quickly, taking him by the hand and tugging him to follow me. I lead him past the break room farther down another hall. I have a better idea…

"Where are we going?"

"Let's go this way," I say as we round a corner and then stop in front of the utility room door. "Because we need some privacy for what I want to do." I pull him inside the dim room that smells of ammonia and lemon and shut us inside. Cleaning supplies, paper products, and light bulbs are stacked from floor to ceiling so there isn't a ton of room, but it'll do. I kick a heavy mop bucket against the door with my foot with the intent to keep out anyone who might have the sudden urge to refill the paper towels during the next fifteen minutes, and then start shimmying out of my silky shorts. The lower half of my uniform consists of black butt shorts over black fishnets and ankle boots, and since I still have to go back out on the floor and finish the rest of my shift after this, I can't risk ripping or tearing anything. Good job thinking ahead for once, girl!

"What are you doing?" Viktor's hazel eyes bounce between me stripping and taking in the contents of the

tiny room I've locked us into. I can tell I've taken him by surprise, but I have a feeling he'll get on board with my plan quickly enough. His eyes have darkened, turned on by my strip show, even if I can't take the time right now to do one properly for him due to my break being only twenty minutes. The small details will get you if you're not careful, and I do not want us to get busted by management.

"Getting naked. You should too because we don't have a lot of time."

"Are we going to fuck in this janitor closet, Red Rocket?"

I nod...slowly after I drop my fishnets carefully atop the growing pile of my outfit for emphasis. "We so are." I drop to my knees in front of him and make quick work of freeing his cock from his jeans. He's already impossibly hard as I stroke him in my hand. His leg muscles flex and his knees buckle just slightly as I take his cock and give it a good lick from base to tip. He groans when I pull him in deep and let him bottom out at the back of my throat. I'm so full with him deep-throating me, but it's good. He's good. And knowing I'm making him feel pleasure gives me a warm feeling inside.

"Sex in the janitor closet was a good idea," Viktor groans as he steadies my head with his hands on either side. He gets quiet then and I know he's watching his cock stroke in and out of my mouth, getting more turned on, and impossibly harder with each slick slide.

Abruptly he stops moving, his cock pulling away as

he bends down to reach for me. "Your mouth feels too fucking good to my cock and I won't last very long with you sucking me like that." Lifting me easily, he turns us so he can rest my back against the wall while he lines his big hard cock up to meet my pussy. I'm soaked and so ready for him that I can't help squirming as he presses just the very tip inside me. "And I need to see your beautiful green eyes looking up into mine when you come shaking all over my cock." I moan against his lips as he sinks his whole glorious length into me, kissing me deeply at the same time, filling me up, holding me close.

God, how I'm going to miss his oh-so-eloquent dirty talking. From the very first, Viktor has been able to say the right words to melt me into a desperate sexual creature helpless to resist him. He has a way with words during sex that hits my sensual switch every single time. Pretty impressive for a guy who's still mastering conversational English, but it's probably part of his charm too. That accent of his paired with his literal word choices becomes Kryptonite for my libido.

Suddenly, I feel irrationally emotional that I won't see him after today for a long time—possibly ever again—and it makes me choke up. I feel my eyes start to water and summon every ounce of strength to fight it off. I will not cry. I will not cry. Instead, I kiss him back and rock my hips into him, urging him to start with the moving.

"Now fuck me goodbye before my break runs out, big man."

Which he proceeded to do. Spectacularly. Especially that last searing look from him as he came. His eyes were so intense as he stared at me pinned to the wall of the utility closet by his cock, my body tingling head to toe from the mind-shattering orgasm he'd just delivered. The intimacy between us was...blinding in that moment.

I hoped I was right about the thoughts roaring and crashing through my head.

Mostly that Viktor didn't want to leave me any more than I wanted him to go—

"Earth to Scarlett."

I'm ripped from my erotic reminiscing quite rudely by Sid with all the finesse of an ice-bucket challenge. Why is Sid Lane even here in the office today? And then I remember...On the guise of dropping in to check out the schedule, he's probably more like checking out his new "friend," Daisy. Yep, those two connected at Pam and Georg's engagement party. While I was doing Viktor up in my room that night, Sid showed up to the party and hit it off with the shy girl.

"I'm right here, Siddy, feet planted firmly on the earth." I wiggle my foot and stomp it on the floor dramatically. "Whatever do you need?" I ask cheerily, desperately trying to distract him from the fact that he knows he just caught me red-handed deep in a filthy sex dream.

At my desk.

In the middle of a PR department.

He laughs and shakes his head. "Um...nothing. But Holly's been trying to get your attention for about two minutes." He pokes his thumb in her direction.

Oh. My. God.

I flush with guilt when I look up to find Holly with her head sticking out of Fiona's office impatiently motioning at me to come and join them.

I move my ass into the office and sit down, trying to peek at Holly out of the corner of my eye. She looks cute. She always looks cute. She's got a tiny little baby bump emerging, but since she's a distance runner, her baby bump looks like someone else's pizza overindulgence.

"Scarlett," Fiona starts, "Holly has something to tell you."

I look at my friend as she flashes me a small smile. "So, you know how Evan and I are having another baby?"

"Yep. How's everything going? Okay?"

She nods. "Yes, great. I'm twelve weeks today, honestly further along than I thought. And I've been thinking that it's been really challenging to be a good wife and a good mom and a good full-time social media manager for the team. Trying to balance it all...it's been wicked hard. And I get these recruitment calls all the time, but I obviously wasn't going to leave and go to another team while Evan is still here."

Fiona taps a pencil on her desk impatiently, clearly wanting Holly to get to the point. She jumps in and says, "Holly's starting her own social media and PR company. She's pulled together a few sports clients who don't have the interest or budget to hire full-time staff, or who want her expertise in campaign planning."

"Wow!" I turn back to Holly. "That's really unexpected."

"I know. It's just that I think if I work from home, I can maybe spend more time with my daughter. With our new baby. I can be more focused on my family and just work when I want, on the projects I want."

I can see she's getting a little emotional, her eyes pooling with tears. I reach out and offer her my hand. "Are you sure you want this?"

She nods and takes my hand in a firm grip. "I've been thinking about it for a while, honestly. Evan is on board. And I really, really love this team, so it's not an easy decision. But I am sure. It's the right thing for me and for my family."

"Well, congratulations then?" It comes out more like a question than I intended, but I'm truly shocked by this news.

"So," Fiona says sharply. "With Holly leaving, I wanted to talk with you about taking on her role and leading our social media efforts."

The shock must be clearly written on my face because Holly jumps in to say, "You did a great job when I was on maternity leave. I can stay another month to on-board you and help you build a plan for the pre-season. And I'm not leaving Vegas. I'll still be here if you need help or advice."

"Are you interested, Scarlett?" Fiona prods my stunned silence.

I think about Viktor, about how badly I want to be with him, about how much he says he wants to be with me. And honestly, I think about saying no. About figuring out something else, about finding a job that will let me see him without the fear of being fired.

But I remember that he's gone for months and he could be lukewarm about things by the time he returns. How can there possibly be a future between me—an uneducated girl who's only known Las Vegas —and a world-renowned Olympic champion and professional athlete who could have any woman he wanted at any time?

When Fiona shows me the new pay scale for this job, my decision is made. I can quit my second job at the casino. I'll be able to do more varied assignments as the social media director. Maybe I can continue to move up within the Crush organization. Maybe I can eventually be something more than what I am today.

"Yes," I finally say. "Yes, I'm interested."

"Great!" Holly says, clapping her hands. "We'll start your training today."

FOR A WEEK STRAIGHT, I work with Holly. She's got a whole folder full of ideas for how to engage the team and fans through social media. She shows me how she budgets the content and how she makes choices about timing. I knew a lot of this from filling in during her maternity leave, but it's good to have a refresher.

We work together on some junior league stuff. There are some hockey clinics and games that we cover together right off the bat. I finally feel as though I'm being stretched to my full potential. This job...fits me.

I really miss Viktor, though. I think about him all the time.

All. The. Time.

I don't want to annoy him, and I don't even know if he would get my texts overseas, but he's on my mind every freaking day. Especially when I'm alone at home like right now. I have no idea how or if my phone plan even works in Russia, and just when I'm about to look that up, a request to FaceTime comes in. *Thank God. I need to hear his voice.*

"Hey!" I answer, waving like a maniac at his image on my phone. Moscow is ten hours ahead of Las Vegas, so even though it's evening for me, his day is just starting. Weird.

"Hello, Red Rocket." Just the sound of his voice makes my body ache with want.

"How is Russia?"

"Russia is fine," he says with a shrug. "Much time in practice. Little time for much else."

"Sounds exhausting but guess what happened here?"

"What?" he asks.

"I got a promotion!"

"That is good, yes?"

"I think so. Holly is leaving to start her own business. She wants to work from home now that she has a second baby coming. So, I got her job."

"Oh," he says, frowning slightly.

"What's that frown all about?"

"I am not expert, but it seems she does a good job."

"She does, and she's got a great reputation with the organization. That's why she can start her own business at, what, like twenty-six? She's getting new job offers every day. This is a really smart move for her. And they seem to think I'll do well at it, too, so… it's an easy decision for me really. I can finally quit my hideous job at the casino."

At this news Viktor nods encouragingly, knowing how much I disliked working there. "I am sure you will be good in your new position. You are very good at *many* things."

"What *many things* are you referring to?" My voice suddenly sounds noticeably huskier.

"Filthy, sexy, pleasurable things." I am rewarded with a lustful-Viktor smile as he answers me. His whole face changes when he smiles and knowing he only does it for me makes it all the better. It's like a secret that only we share.

I laugh. "No need to beat around the bush."

"I do not understand this. What do you mean?"

Still giggling, I shake my head. "No worries. Are you hoping to just jump right into the phone sex, then? No small talk needed?"

"If you require small talk, then we will talk," he answers. "However, I would like to talk while watching you touch yourself."

For whatever reason, this cracks me up. Viktor looks totally confounded by my laughter. Still, I pull my T-shirt over my head and my pajama bottoms off. This gets a smile out of him.

"Yes," he cheers. "I have been dreaming of those tits, Red Rocket. I dream of putting them in my mouth, of rolling those hard nipples under my tongue. I've dreamed of touching the soft skin underneath, of smelling your sweet skin."

Boy, he does own the market on dirty talk. I tweak my already-hard nipples between my thumb and forefinger, making sure to show Viktor. He groans and shows me how he's stroking himself. This turns me on. So much.

I pull my vibrator from my nightstand and switch it on, making sure that Viktor sees how I hold it against my aching clit. I sit the phone on the nightstand, propped up against the lamp, and use both hands, spreading myself wide and flexing my hip muscles forward.

"Yes," Viktor urges. "Yes, Scarlett. Focus. Think of me, hard and hot in you. Think of my cock buried deep, my tongue assaulting your sweet clit. Take all I have to give you, Red Rocket. Take it."

"I'm coming." I manage to breathe as an orgasm takes me. It's not as strong as the ones I've had when he's really been inside of me, but it still feels good, still floods my body with lovely tingling endorphins.

"Look at me, Scarlett," he orders.

I do, and he's widened the shot, so I can see him finish, so I can see his face when he comes. It's as hot and intense as only Viktor can make it.

After, I lie in bed while we talk, which is something else I've missed. Viktor and I had a lot of sex, but the post-coital chats are what made our friendship grow. And in many respects, I can see why he asked for physical release before we talked. We're both relaxed. Sated. *Calm.* I like this man. He talks about his team and their grueling practices. I talk about some of the work I'm doing. It's idle chatter. Normal conversation. The first we've really had, I suppose, and I want more of it. I wonder if he does too.

He says he'll call again soon. And then, "I miss you, Scarlett. More than I expected."

My breath catches. "I...I miss you too, Viktor."

We hang up and then I'm smiling and crying at the same time. I fall asleep like that.

He surprises me again by calling the very next night. And the next. This becomes a normal occurrence for us, and while we don't always have phone sex, I do send him plenty of naughty pictures. He reciprocates, though his pictures are often more funny than sexy, because he's slightly technologically inept. I think it's adorable though.

One night, he casually suggests I visit him in Russia.

"But I don't even have a passport. Doesn't that take a long time to get?"

"Everyone should have passport. Go get one. Then we will plan a visit."

"I don't even know if I can take a vacation," I tell him. "I'd have to clear it with Fiona and—"

"Just go get it started, Scarlett. Call Saul and he will get it done for you." He cutely rolls his eyes at me. "No excuses."

I MUST ADMIT Viktor's proposal that I go to Russia this summer got me excited enough to get the process started the very next day. When I call the number on the card Viktor left with me to set up an appointment, I'm greeted with, "Miss Woods, we've been expecting your call, good morning. You'll need to come to the office with your birth certificate—today if possible."

Oh-kay then. I guess I'll be heading downtown during my lunch break today. I take down the directions, thank the secretary, and hang up, thinking it's super weird that they addressed me by name when I called.

But the weirdness didn't end there.

Turns out Saul Heisenberg's office is inside the old Golden Gate Hotel on Fremont Street behind a nail salon within the casino shops. Bizarre. But then his line of work is kind of bizarre so I guess it shouldn't be such a surprise to me where he keeps his office.

Aaaand in unconventional style I'm met out front by a truly enormous tree trunk of a man sporting a burgundy plaid shirt and the sweetest smile I've ever seen. He introduces himself as Huell and tells me to follow him back. If Huell wasn't so kindly, I don't think I would follow him anywhere, let alone into some weird office in the back of a casino on Fremont Street where I might never be seen or heard of again.

But there you have it. We all do things we might not think we'd ever do because the desire outweighs the risk. Sometimes you have to take a chance. So here I am meeting Saul-the-Fixer at his weird office location to help me get a passport...because Viktor asked me to. I guess at some point in this freaky experience I decided that I wish to visit Viktor more than I care to worry about what exactly a *fixer* in Las Vegas has among his job description.

I wouldn't even want to guess at this point...

Saul is forty-ish with thinning hair, wearing a suit I would place firmly in the purple category, and throwing out a I-can-handle-anything attitude. What did I expect from a guy who has a personal assistant in the form of a giant bodyguard with no neck? I'd be super confident too if I had a Huell guarding me all the time.

But I will say that he gets shit done. And fast.

Within fifteen minutes, Saul has my passport pictures taken and the information filled out on the forms awaiting my signature. He tells me he'll have the process expedited and my passport in ten days or less. When I ask him how much for the expediting services, he tells me it's already been taken care of. How in the hell did Viktor meet this guy? The extra help is quite nice.

No less than one minute after being escorted back through to the casino by the kindly Huell, my phone pings with a text from Pam. The Kolochevs have returned from their island honeymoon all tanned and in full newlywed glory. It's sweet...kind of.

Pam: Lunch today? I've got news.

Scarlett: Can't. I already used my lunch break applying for a passport.

Pam: Why?

Scarlett: Viktor wants me to visit him in Russia.

Pam: Whoa. That's big news.

Scarlett: I know. It's not for sure yet though.

Scarlett: What's your news?

Pam: Well…maybe we can visit
Russia together…

Scarlett: Why?!

Pam: Because Georg was asked to
play summer league, too.

Scarlett: Whoa! How do you feel
about that?

Pam: Not sure yet. But we'll work
it out!

Scarlett: Okay. Well, drinks soon?

Pam: Yes. ASAP!!

Damn. Just married and he's off to Russia for the rest of the summer. Now I can't feel too badly for myself. Viktor and I barely know each other.

So why do I feel so crazy excited at the very remote prospect of seeing him again soon?

One week later.

"SO THAT WILL BE your main assignment this summer," Fiona says with her usual sharpness laced with a totally fake smile. "You must have some big friends in high places to get such a long assignment so soon after starting in a brand-new position, but I suppose social media coverage of our European players and their summer programs is good for building the Crush brand worldwide. We have Georg and Viktor and the guys from our minor league affiliate there as well, so I want you to focus on them first. I also want anything and everything that can be promoted to elevate our team and their place in the sport of hockey. Revisiting historical places and events are always popular, so keep an eye out for any possible series you could put together. Photos, lots and lots of photos, Scarlett. We've got your disclaimer filled out for restrictions on taking shots of any government buildings, police, etc. Just sign and date it. And I'll be interfacing with you on anything that needs attention here locally. You can post from Russia as well as Vegas so the summer feeds can still go out as normal. It's light in the off-season anyway..."

Fiona babbles on and on as I sit stunned in her office—yet again—at how unbelievably crazy it is that she's called me in here to inform me I'll be heading off to Russia for a month-long PR assignment representing the team. Oh, and I'm leaving in just under a week. Jesus. I have quickly learned that stepping into Fiona's office can be a helluva dangerous operation, so tread fucking carefully.

It's a good thing Saul's office left me a voice mail earlier that my passport arrived.

I'm going to need it a lot sooner than I ever

expected because this travel thing is happening soon, and I have eleventy-million things to do to get ready.

And Viktor has been a busy, busy boy with all the secret plans and not telling me. I'm going to have to show him just how annoyed *and* appreciative I am when we FaceTime tonight.

The big, sexy, adorable, jerk.

21
we need two cars

Scarlett

Federal Centre of Sport Training
Novogorsk, Russia

My belly is flip-flopping like crazy as we make our way off the plane. Pam is jabbering on the phone to Georg and my eyes are darting around the place, taking in the total strangeness of being in a country halfway around the world.

"The guys are down in baggage claim," Pam announces as she finishes her call. "They have two cars waiting."

"Why do we need two cars?"

Pam's eyebrow goes up in response, her expression telling me precisely why we'll be needing two *separate* cars.

"Oh." How could I forget those two are still in honeymoon mode? They won't be delayed for the time it takes to ride from the airport to the athlete's village before they start banging. It's cute, really it is.

"It's interesting how much this looks like every other airport while also looking completely different," Pam comments. "There's a McDonalds. Weird, right?"

"I guess? I'm not very well traveled."

We walk and walk, following the signs until we find the escalator to take us down to the baggage claim level. And there, finally, is my Viktor. He's wearing a black leather jacket and jeans and damn, he's delicious. He's also wearing something of a grin on his handsome face. Not a full-on smile in public (obviously) but he wears it well. Especially because that grin is directed right at me. God, I've missed him so much more than I ever imagined.

Pam runs for Georg, practically knocking him over as she jumps into his arms, her legs around his waist, her mouth on his. No matter that there are hundreds of other people around to see their show. They're in their own personal PDA bubble and one hundred percent oblivious to the rest of the world.

Viktor holds out a hand, which I take, feeling suddenly shy. He pulls me close, his strong arms suddenly around me, my head on his chest. We just hug for a moment. It feels like home and that realization makes my heart take on an erratic beat. I don't know what I expected when I saw Viktor again, but this feeling inside me surprises me greatly. I do care about him...a lot. But could it be more than that?

"See you back at the ranch," Georg says in our general direction, taking Pam's hand and walking off toward the baggage carousel. Our luggage seems to be offloading, so Viktor motions that we should go that way, as well.

Baggage collected; Viktor holds my hand as we walk outside to a waiting town car. He says something in Russian to the driver who nods and pushes a button to give us privacy. I'm too amped up, too nervous to feel sexy right now. Viktor must sense it, too. He takes his seat, shuts the door and we take off, driving for a few minutes in silence before he says anything.

"I am glad you are here," he finally says, taking my hand again.

"Me too. How has it been so far?"

"It has been good. I do a charity thing each summer while I am in Russia. I hope to show you."

"A charity thing?"

"Yes, I don't know if I have told you that I lost my father when I was fifteen. He was my coach and when he died in an automobile accident, a local charity reached out to my mother to offer additional coaching for me. They were a feeder to the Russian Junior Hockey League and I very desperately wanted to play there. It changed my life, of course. So, I like to come back and work with the kids in the program each summer."

My heart melts a little at this. "That is really sweet. I had no idea you were helping kids like that."

"I know it might be hard to believe. Many people think I am asshole and incapable of being kind."

"Well, I can personally attest that you can be very kind, but this is more than that. Not everyone would think to go back and pay forward the opportunities they've had. Can I take some pictures of you working with the kids while I'm here? Do a little side story on your charity work?"

"I think it would be okay but will have to clear with the charity."

"Of course."

It's quiet between us again. Viktor's thumb rubs against my hand as I bite my cheek, trying to think of what to talk about. I finally settle on, "I've really missed you, Viktor. A lot more than I thought I would."

I turn and he looks at me with a softness that I'm not sure I've seen from him before. "I feel the same, Red Rocket."

"You know what I thought when I hugged you back at the airport?"

"That it was very awkward to have Georg and Pamela making out right beside us?"

This makes me laugh out loud. "You got jokes, boy?"

Viktor's lips twitch and his eyes twinkle. He's clearly delighted to have made me laugh. That's his delighted face.

"I do agree. That was awkward for sure, but actually, my thoughts were more along the lines of feeling like I was at home. You make me feel like I'm home. Is that weird?"

"Is not weird. I feel it, as well."

I sigh happily as Viktor leans in for a soft kiss. That familiar desire blooms easily as I lean into him. Suddenly, I'm very thankful for the partition between us and the driver. Very thankful indeed.

Viktor

WE PULL into the athlete's village at the Federal Centre of Sport Training in Novogorsk, just outside of Moscow. The driver helps us to unload Scarlett's bags while she looks around the simple little "town square," perplexed.

"I think I'm supposed to stay in an apartment with two other women. They work in the cafeteria or something?" She pulls out her phone to confirm.

I clear my throat and wait until she looks up at me. "I hope you don't mind. I know it is presumptuous, but I thought you might like to stay with me."

Scarlett's lips open just slightly. Then she bites on the lower one, shy about the offer I've just made.

"It is okay if you think it is too soon. And the space is not big. I requested an apartment in the area where married couples and families stay. They gave me only the smallest apartment but have agreed you can stay with me if you would like."

She gives me a soft smile and nods. "Okay. Yes. Sure."

I can't help but smile in return. I pick up her suitcase and we start the short walk.

My apartment is basically a living and dining area, a small bedroom with a double bed, and a bathroom. I am a big man and I barely fit on the bed alone, so sleeping in it with two people will be interesting, but I want Scarlett near me. I don't want to spend another night away from her.

She looks around as we shove inside, and it is very hard to read her thoughts.

"It's very…beige," she finally says.

"Yes. They don't allow adornments as it is only temporary housing."

"I see. Well, it'll be fine."

"It is small."

"It is. And you are large. But it's going to be ours while I'm here, so that'll be fun."

I nod. "Speaking of fun. I have some things to show you. Would you like to take a walk with me?"

"I need to clean up a little. And maybe take a short nap. Would you be okay with me finding you in a little bit?"

I nod and lean down to kiss her forehead. "Of course. Actually, I have a fight later. You can walk down and see it. I will write the directions, but it is easy."

"A fight?" Scarlett's face is a mask of surprise.

"Sometimes the guys do MMA fighting here to let off steam."

"MMA? Wow. I knew you liked to bet on the fights, but I didn't realize you fought yourself. You don't get enough of it on the ice?"

"MMA is a strategy game. It is all about controlled aggression. You will like it."

"You think I'll like watching you get pummeled? I doubt it."

I lean in and place a kiss on her sweet lips. "You will love it."

Scarlett

I WAKE up a couple of hours later, worried I've missed Viktor's fight. But there's a note on the kitchen counter with a lanyard pass that I assume will allow me entry into the fight, and I still have time. I head out after a five-minute shower and a change of clothes, following the map he drew for me to a warehouse-looking building just a few blocks away.

The sound of cheering tells me I'm in the right place. The guy at the door waves me in and I slip inside, standing in the back of the crowd. There are two men I don't recognize in the ring right now. A man beside me yells, "Kick his ass, Popov!" so I at least know he speaks English. I ask him if Viktor has already fought.

"Demoskev? He won his first fight. He will fight again after this one."

"Okay, thanks."

Living in Vegas my whole life with a dad like mine, I've certainly seen a few MMA fights. Usually lower-level ones with dirty fighters and even dirtier managers. This fight, though, is more about skill, I notice. The fighters are both obviously athletes, and if I had to guess, they'd probably be in deep crap if they got hurt cage fighting when they have multi-million-dollar contracts awaiting them after the summer.

The guy named Popov easily wins his fight, making his opponent tap out with an arm bar in the second round. My neighbor cheers loudly and makes sure to tell everyone he's up a hundred bucks.

"You want to place bet?" the guy asks me. "On Demoskev?"

"What are the odds?" I ask warily.

"Twenty-to-one now. Minimum bet is twenty dollars US."

I pull a twenty from my pocket and hand it to him. He grins and writes my first name down in a little notebook, winking at me as he leaves to go take bets from others.

Viktor comes out, a hulking, sweaty beast of a man, shirtless and wearing just a pair of basketball shorts. He's really such a glorious being to look at. His face is serious as he slips a mouth guard in and pounds one fist into the opposite palm. His opponent is shorter but stocky. He looks thick and muscular.

And mean. He sneers at Viktor, who just keeps his head up and his focus laser sharp.

The first round starts with the opponent, someone the guys call Rybakov, going full out with a series of punches. Viktor seems to be holding back, blocking easily, moving in a circle to avoid getting pinned against the cage.

I'm fascinated by how he moves. He's a brick on the ice, unmovable unless he wants to be moved. Here, he almost dances with his opponent, his movement thoughtful, graceful. Every muscle ripples with tension, a coil ready to be sprung. It's quite a sight and I suddenly wish I'd brought my camera. It also begs the question why Viktor can be so light on his feet in the ring, but have no skill on the dance floor.

It's easy to see that Rybakov's plan is to come out as aggressively as possible. He punches and kicks, most of it not really making much of an impact on Viktor. He gets in a few clean hits, which I assume Viktor has allowed. My sense is that he's trying to let the guy use all of his energy, only for Viktor to be fully primed to take him down. He's playing with his food.

They head into round two and Viktor has barely even taken a swing. Rybakov is breathing heavily, having expended an awful lot of energy. I can see Rybakov's punches are getting sloppy. His kicks aren't as high or as targeted. And Viktor sees it too, because he comes out of his shell, defense turning to offense as he jabs, right, right left, uppercut. Rybakov staggers back, having taken every single one of those punches. He's dazed, a fact that Viktor takes advantage of with a roundhouse kick that sends the poor guy sprawling back against the cage. They get in a tussle, wrapped up in each other, as Viktor's body slams the guy and gets him twisted like a pretzel. The arm bar is tight, and I can see Rybakov's face go red as he struggles against the sheer size and strength of his opponent.

It's over a minute later and the two shake hands as Viktor takes the win. I cheer, wildly turned on by the way he controlled that whole fight. He was right; I loved it. What does it say about me that I'm hot for a guy who just beat the crap out of another guy?

The bookie guy from earlier comes around and asks me if I want to bet again. I shake my head and he hands me a stack of twenties, which I accept with a big grin before heading off to find my man to the side of the octagon. He's toweling off some of the sweat but pulls me close for a kiss before I can object. It's long and sexy and I don't care that people are watching.

"You were great out there." I breathe as we pull apart.

"It helped knowing you were watching."

"I doubt it," I say. "I think you would have won, regardless. But it was still sexy."

He grins and pulls on a T-shirt. "How much did you win?"

"I only bet twenty, but the odds were twenty-to-one, so I pocketed a big wad of cash. Dinner is on me tonight."

"Dinner and dancing?" he asks, grabbing his gym bag and slinging it over his arm.

"Only if you shower first."

"Only if you are there to watch." The naughty smirk he adds on is an extra cute touch.

"Look at you with all the witty jokes. The Mad Russian has found his funny side." I throw my own smirk right back his way.

"It is easy to make jokes and tease with you, Red Rocket. Now that you are here, I cannot seem to help myself. Please don't tell anyone I am funny and ruin my longstanding bad reputation," he says with a completely straight face. I think he's being deadly serious.

This man kills me.

Viktor

"YOU LOOK VERY BEAUTIFUL."

Scarlett's hair is braided and hanging over one shoulder. She wears a black tank top, jeans, and high-heeled shoes. She looks down at herself and shrugs. "Thanks. I feel underdressed. I didn't bring a lot of nice clothes."

"You are perfect."

"Well, you look pretty darn good yourself, mister.

Remember that time you put on a tux just to take it off again?"

My lips twitch and so does my cock. "I really want to show you the city tonight."

"Sexy plans thwarted. Dang."

"Only postponed."

"Were you serious about dancing? Because do I need to remind you that you are a very terrible dancer?"

"Come on." I will not dignify an answer, but Scarlett snickers, nonetheless.

We head out and Scarlett seems curious to see a line of taxi cabs just outside the village gates. We get in one and I give the driver an address.

At the restaurant, I help Scarlett order from the menu, which is written in Russian, of course, and then she asks me about the fights.

"What about them?"

"How often do you do the actual fighting?"

"Not very often. A few times a year."

"Why?"

I shrug. "I enjoy the strategy of it."

"I can see that. You definitely had a plan. That guy burned all of his energy in the first round then all you had to do was strike."

"It is often like that in amateur fighting," I explain. "These are hockey players, but they are used to the pace on the ice. In fighting, it is different. It requires thinking differently. They do not adjust but I do."

"Why do you fight so much on the ice?"

"It is about throwing your opponent off balance. I leverage my size against them, and they get angry. When they fight, they are off-kilter and it makes them play less strategically. Also, the crowd enjoys a good fight once in a while."

"People used to say you were a dirty player, though. That you tried to hurt people."

"I did sometimes. I am not proud of who I was before. This change has been good for me."

"I'm glad you came to Vegas, if only because I wouldn't have met you if you hadn't."

"I am glad also. For that reason and many others."

"I never thought," she starts to say. "It's just that..." She sighs.

"What is it, Red Rocket?"

"It's hard to believe you can find something again, you know? After you've lost someone? I have to pinch myself to remind myself that this is real. That we're here together, having this adventure."

"Scarlett, somehow I feel that the stars would have aligned for us, regardless. In a million years, I could not have imagined being in love with an American girl who visited me in Russia. But here we are, and I feel that it was meant to be. Is that sounding very silly?"

Scarlett's eyes go wide and then she smiles and looks down at the table. "No. Not at all silly. It's sweet. You're sweet to me all the time."

We eat and talk about Scarlett's travel from the

States, then head to a famous bar called Coyote Ugly. It's based on a real place in America where the people get up on the top of the bar and dance. Scarlett tells me there is also a Coyote Ugly in Las Vegas inside the New York-New York casino, but she has never seen the movie.

Indeed, when we arrive, there are women dancing on top of the bar. We get drinks and watch for a while, but it is loud and crowded and Scarlett is not wrong—I am a very bad dancer. Still, I pull her to her feet, and we sway together to a song I don't recognize. Scarlett seems to know it, though, and she hums the tune as we dance, our bodies aligned in a way that makes me want her badly. I cannot help that my cock wakes up from rubbing against her soft curves.

"Fighting in hockey is a little like this sometimes. An awkward dance," I say in her ear.

"Only you probably don't want to fuck your opponent." She smiles up at me.

I push against her a little. "I like it when you say dirty things. Say that word again, Scarlett."

"Fuck," she breathes.

"I want that very much. To fuck you. To feel you. To taste you."

"Well, if the goal is to make me feel off balance, it's working."

Suddenly, I can't wait a moment longer. My lips meet hers urgently as I claim her in a wild kiss in the middle of a public dance floor. I have admitted I love her, and I think she feels the same. I know that I want her to feel the same, but I can't push her to say something she may not be ready to tell me. I did not lie. Vegas has changed me. Scarlett has changed me. But perhaps, being away from her, not having as much...access to her has been the largest change. Even when Paulina, my ex, was away from me, I never felt the same yearning. As if I'd lost my *rodstvennaya dusha*. My mate for my soul.

Hockey is still my focus, but my heart has opened for Scarlett. I want nothing more than to be close to her. As close as it is possible for two people to be. I need to be inside her, making her come, giving her pleasure until she can't take anymore.

Without a word, I take her hand and lead her out into the night. I hail a taxi and we spend the entire drive back to the village making out. I love kissing her. I can't ever seem to get enough of her kisses.

I pick her up, her legs around my waist, and carry her into the apartment. It's not the most romantic of environments, but I don't care. She doesn't care. I unlock the door and kick it back shut once we're inside.

Scarlett's feet hit the carpet and she asks for just a minute, slipping inside the bathroom. I don't want to be away from her, though, so I push open the door and find her brushing her teeth. The space is too small for two people, but I crowd her. I stand right behind her, my arms on either side of the sink, caging her in. Her breathing becomes uneven, her eyes darkening as she looks at me in the mirror. My cock is so hard, and I am not in the least bit shy about letting her feel it against her ass. She finishes brushing, rinses, and then stares at me. It's a willful look she wears, a dare.

I lean forward and kiss along the back of her neck. Her head falls back, allowing me more access. I back off only enough to allow her to turn and face me, my hand pushing her tank top pulling her heavy breast from her bra. It spills over the material and I kiss and lick and suckle the hard nipple as Scarlett sighs, a satisfied moan spilling from her throat.

"This is a very tiny bathroom." she breathes.

"The bed is also very small." I groan. "But we will manage."

We take the few steps to the bedroom, Scarlett pulling her shirt over her head as I work the clasp on her bra. Her breasts are so perfect. I hold them in my hands and pay them great attention as she arches into me. I get lost in their heaviness, in the way her hard nipples feel against my tongue, in the moans of desire that come with every nip and bite and pinch.

My mouth moves down to her belly as I unbutton her jeans and slip them down, helping her step free before allowing my hands to explore her inner thighs. She spreads her legs, an invitation, her body bare to me now. I touch and caress as much of her as I can, pleased when her skin erupts in gooseflesh. When my mouth finds her cunt, she sags against me with a sigh.

"Yes," she says. "Yes, please. Please."

I kiss and lick, my tongue flicking at her clit, my fingers parting her folds and finding her sweet pussy wet and willing. I finger her until she cries out, sucking her clit until the clench of her cunt around my fingers shows proof of her satisfaction.

We move slightly as I push her to the bed, pulling my clothing off, stroking my cock so she can see how hard and ready I am. She watches with hooded eyes, her fingers playing idly at her nipples, her red hair now loose from its braid, wild around her like fire.

"Open your legs wide, Red Rocket. Let me see you."

She spreads her legs so wide and I take in the sight of her swollen pussy, glistening with desire, ready for the taking. I kiss her there one more time before moving to kiss her lips. Our tongues mingle as I let her taste what I taste. I tell her over and over how good she is, how much I want her. When I push inside, she cries out, her fingertips digging into my back.

"I've missed you," she says. "God, I've missed you so much. Fuck me. Make it hard. Make me yours."

"Say it again," I growl.

"Fuck me, Viktor. Take me. Fuck me. Hard. Fast. I need it so badly."

I won't last long like this. I've imagined this since the day I left, and I want to make it last forever. But Scarlett gets what Scarlett wants when it comes to this. So I fuck her, hard and fast. Her gorgeous tits bounce as she reaches back for the headboard. I watch every expression on her face and when her eyes close and her breathing halts; I know the telltale clench will come next. She comes and comes and then I am coming, too and neither of us breathes while we disappear into our collective pleasure.

When I collapse on top of her, she strokes the bare skin of my back and kisses my cheek. It's a long time before I can will myself to roll away from her, and I find her already asleep. She curls into a ball on her side and I wrap myself around her, skin to skin, never wanting to let go.

Yes, I believe I am truly in love with this woman.

And I want nothing more than to give her the world.

22
clear as mud

Scarlett

A week into my trip and I'm finally finding my legs in a foreign country. My days are full of work on the off-season stories like Fiona and I arranged, and my nights are full of Viktor. It's a fantastic combination for me—something I could totally get used to. Today, Pam and I are watching the guys practice. I take a ton of photos and make notes for our social media feeds, reviewing periodically to see if I'm getting anything I can use.

"These are really good shots," Pam comments over my shoulder. She holds her cup of to-die-for Russian coffee in both hands. Its official name is Raf coffee, but I have no idea what that means. Viktor told me it's made with espresso and cream and vanilla sugar that's been caramelized, then topped with whipped cream (of course) to make it just that bit more decadent. It's divine and I'm going to have to learn how to make it once I'm home because I'm not giving it up. "You could have potential as a photographer, you know. Have you ever thought of pursuing photography, Scarlett?"

"Really?" I look back through the photos, pleased at the compliment. I've never thought of myself as a photographer, but these are some remarkable shots. There are some silly ones, some action ones, and a few that show some tension and discord between players. I'm so thankful Viktor arranged for consent and permission from the facility.

"Really," Pam confirms. "I could see these blown up and shown in an art gallery. They tell a story."

"Wow. Thanks. You just made my day, friend."

"Happy to help," she replies in typical, no-nonsense, tell-it-like-it-is Pam fashion.

I set aside the camera and watch for a while, enjoying my Russian coffee and the view of Viktor on the ice. Pam's face is so serene as she watches Georg. I'm fascinated by how much love she shows in her facial expressions alone.

"So it must be good to be back with Georg," I comment.

"It's amazing. The apartment is, like, the size of my bathroom at home, but still...I was not looking forward to spending the summer without him."

"I hear you," I agree.

"And how are things with Viktor?"

"Good."

"Well that's vague." She rolls her eyes at me.

"I mean, what else do you want me to tell you?" I shoot back.

"The guy pulled serious strings to get you here. I'm thinking it must be better than just plain ole good. If you flew halfway around the world for 'good' then I think your standards are too low."

I take a deep breath and then let it out, a little bit of a laugh escaping with it. "Well, the sex is amazing. We, umm, snuck in here one night and we might have done it on the bleachers."

"That's exciting. I'm impressed."

I shake my head. "He's amazing in bed."

"And?"

"And he's really pretty sweet. He's very good to me."

"Do you love him?" Pam asks softly.

"I don't know. Maybe? He said something the other night...about being in love with an American girl. It freaked me out a little to be honest."

"He did?" Pam's eyes are as wide as saucers.

"He didn't say 'I love you' or anything, but he said he'd never imagined he'd be here in Russia, in love with an American girl."

"And what was your response?"

"It was while we were out at dinner and he caught me off guard. I wasn't expecting him to just come out with the L-word, but really, it's pretty much how he says everything. Being direct is not something Viktor struggles with. I wasn't sure how to respond. So, I told him he was sweet and then we were interrupted by the waiter arriving with our order... and then we ate our food."

Pam laughs out loud then covers her mouth with one hand. "You totally left him hanging?"

"I guess," I say with a shrug. "We went out and had a great time after that. We had scorching hot sex when we got home. Everything's been really wonderful since I've been here."

"Well, you can't just leave a thing like that out there. I mean, have you even talked about what this thing is between the two of you?"

"Nope." I shake my head. "It's always been about sexual attraction. We're super compatible that way. We talk and stuff, but we're still getting to know each other. And I don't equate sex with love. I think we need more time."

"Do you think he equates sex with love?" Pam asks.

"Are you being Dr. Phil today, or what?"

"I'm just curious. Like I said, a guy doesn't bring a girl around the world just for a quick screw."

I give Pam the *you're starting to be obnoxious* look, hoping she'll take the hint and stop interrogating me. "I don't think either of us think of it as a quickie thing. But we also haven't defined it. He's not been in a relationship in a long time, and I'm still kind of messed up about Stephen, so..."

"Well, there are a million reasons I came up with for why Georg and I couldn't work. And the same for Holly and Evan. When it's meant to be, we have to let it be."

I sit and think about this for a minute. I mean, who am I to know what's meant to be? Viktor is not someone I would ever have seen myself with. He had such a dark reputation when he came to the Crush. He seemed so serious, so stoic. Even violent and occasionally dangerous. But I've seen a softer side of him, a side that laughs and smiles. A side that cares about others and shows a great deal of generosity. I'll never forget how he arranged for Saul to help me if anyone threatened me while he was away. And I wonder if the real Viktor just got sidetracked by coaches and athletics and competition. I wonder if he shut down his heart after it got broken, and if maybe I'm just the lucky one helping him to get it started up again.

And what about me? I live in fear every day. Every. Day. I try to project confidence, self-assurance, independence. But I worry about my safety. I worry about money. I have a hard time accepting love or kindness without expecting to be let down. And these feelings are so tied up with Stephen and my father...

How can I just let that go? How do I release myself from those burdens that have been a part of my life for years?

How can I ever really open myself up to anyone, Viktor or otherwise?

As I'm mulling all this over, a group of shady-looking men dressed in slick suits catch my eye at the far end of the rink. Could they be here about some government photo restrictions?

One of them looks vaguely familiar and...oh—

As we make eye contact, I see his mouth curl into a half-smile that chills me to the bone. That cold fear fills my veins, all too familiar from the days when gangsters showed up at our apartment, ready to hurt people in order to collect on gambling debts.

They survey the practice for a while and then leave. No harm. No interaction. But for a hideous five minutes, my heart nearly beat itself out of my chest. Shock-still the whole time, I just stare at the ice, trying not to pay any attention to them. Only when they leave do I take a steadying breath.

I make some excuse about needing to get back to my laptop to edit the images and get them posted. Pam gives me a side hug and goes back to watching her husband with rapt attention. As I scurry toward the door, trying to get a better look at the guy I thought I recognized, I'm stopped by a random employee, who tells me in broken English that someone left "this" for me.

In his hand is a thumb drive.

I hold it like it might explode, between two fingertips, held away from my body as if it might contaminate me. Dread sits like a rock in the pit of my stomach. Is this what I've been expecting since Stephen's death? Another threat, a blackmail attempt...whatever it is, it can't be good. No way. I've worked two jobs, lived very frugally, just because I thought this day would come. Just because I knew that some day, Stephen's debts, my father's debts, would get handed down to me.

I make the short walk back to the apartment and I don't think I take one breath all the way. My heart feels like it might beat itself right out of my chest and my hands shake as I unlock the door.

I sit, my hand hovering over the laptop for a long time before I finally talk myself into opening it, into sliding the innocuous little piece of technology into the slot.

There is only one file on the drive. A video.

The tears start the minute I press "play."

Stephen's face, grainy but recognizable, in our old apartment, in front of his laptop. He looks over his shoulder a few times. He takes a deep breath.

I forget sometimes. So wrapped up in fear and anger at being abandoned, I forget how much I miss him sometimes. He had bright blue eyes and jet-black hair. He was gorgeous in that way that made women take second and third looks. But he was with me, and I only had to share him with his addictions. He was my best friend, the man I wanted to do life with. Until he was gone.

His life was so wasted. It makes me sick with sadness to think of him now, seeing his face in a way I haven't in a couple of years now. When he speaks, my heart just breaks all over again.

"Scar," he says. "I don't...I don't know how much time I have. I hate what I've put you through. Hate that you've suffered because of me. But I need you to know some things. I know you love your dad. I love him too, like my own father. And I know what you've sacrificed in your life. For him. Because of him. For me. Because of me."

He trails off, taking another deep breath in, then letting it out with a puff of his cheeks. He runs a hand through his curly hair.

"I didn't mean for all of this to happen. He needed help. Needed help with his debts and his legal issues and he didn't want to hurt you. And I didn't want to hurt you. But we both did anyway. But he's not dead, Scar. Your dad...he's...I paid his debts. It's why I got so far in. Because I took the fall for his debts, so you two could leave it behind for good."

I hear banging on the door behind him. His eyes go wide as he turns and yells something in Russian. *He spoke Russian?* What the fuck? I want so badly to reach through the screen, to help him, to save him. I know what's coming. I know where this is headed. I was in the hospital and he was about to die. And the last thing he did was try to speak to me.

I'm sobbing messily, loudly, as he leans closer to the screen. He turns and yells again in Russian. His speech is faster as he finishes.

"Your dad is in Russia. He told me he'd have to leave for a while, to protect you. Scar...I love you, so much. I'm so sorry, baby."

He takes one last longing-filled glance at the screen. It's like he can see me now, through time and space and death and life.

And then his laptop lid shuts, and the screen goes black.

23

dreams and revelations

Viktor

I walk into the apartment and find Scarlett nearly catatonic at the kitchen table, her laptop open in front of her, her face streaked with tears.

"Scarlett?"

She turns and it's impossible for me to read the emotions I see on her face. Fear, certainly. Panic. Sickness. Sadness. It is overwhelming.

"Red Rocket?" I ask, my voice hitching upward awkwardly.

"My...this guy...he left a thumb drive. And Stephen..." Scarlett's eyes flicker back and forth like she's trying to process. She lets out a breath.

"Is this about you taking photos? Take your time," I say, kneeling in front of her. "Just tell me from the beginning."

She shakes her head no and thinks for a minute, her hand going to her chest like she might be trying to claw her heart out. Or hold it inside. I'm not sure which.

Scarlett explains again about her ex-fiancé who died suspiciously. She tells me how she's never really thought he killed himself, not willingly. She talks about her father, who wasn't the most law-abiding American citizen, who also had a gambling addiction, and who has been missing and presumed dead for years.

"Someone's been watching me," she says, her hands shaking. I take them in mine and nod for her to continue. "For a long time. I kind of knew it, suspected it. I worried they'd come for his debts, you know? And every day that they didn't sort of let me believe falsely that all of this was over. That I might be able to move on."

"And you cannot?" I ask.

"My dad's not dead, Viktor." She lets out a nearly hysterical laugh. "He's here in Russia. And some guy found me in the arena today and handed me this thumb drive with a video of Stephen. His last words were to me before they came for him. He paid off my dad's debts, and sent him packing. And Stephen died paying for that."

We talk for a long time, moving to the couch, where I pull her close, my arm around her shoulder, her head on my chest. She tells me that she just knew that Stephen hadn't killed himself. What she didn't know was that much of his descent into addiction was caused by his attempt to get her father out of debt, free from the threat of violence.

"I've been so angry at him for so long," Scarlett says through her tears. "My dad. Mad at him for abandoning me. And Stephen?"

"I am sorry you have been so hurt by these people you have loved," I say. It is all I can think to say.

"It makes it really hard for me, you know?" she asks. "I've just...I've been trying to be on my own, you know? I just..."

I stroke her long, red hair. On a whim, I lean in and kiss her temple. "You do not have to be alone, Red Rocket," I say. "I am here now."

"I can't promise I'll be any good for you," she says, tears falling again. "What if I'm ruined?"

"Ruined?" I ask. "This confuses me. Why should you feel ruined?"

"For love," she says, almost a whisper.

I am shocked to hear this, though I realize quickly I should not be. I, too, have closed off my heart. To avoid the hurt again, perhaps. To allow myself to not be distracted from my athletic goals, definitely.

"I don't believe that you are ruined," I say. "Though I understand why you worry about this. I understand, because I worry, too, that I will not be good for you. It is worth trying, though. You are worth the trying. And I will wait for you for as long as you need."

She's quiet for a long time, so long that I start to wonder if I have said something wrong. Just as I start to ask her for her thoughts, she says, "You know, Viktor, you can be a little bit swoony sometimes."

"Swoony? What is this?"

She laughs lightly. "Sexy, sweet, making my stomach have the butterflies."

"Oh," I say.

Scarlett turns to look at me, her mouth set in a lopsided grin. Her eyes still look sad, but she's so beautiful. Butterflies in the stomach, I think I understand.

She traces her fingertip over my lips. "That frown. So cute."

I pull her closer, my lips touching hers. It's not a kiss for sex—no, it is something different. I do not know how to put words to it, but it feels like a promise of something more.

We pull away and I have an idea.

"Scarlett, would you allow me to do some research? Perhaps we can find your father?"

"Your shady suit guys?" she asks.

"I know people, yes."

"I would...yes, I would like that, I think."

"Yes. Okay." I get up, reluctant to let her go, but I want to find Scarlett's father. It feels urgent and important.

I call Vlad and ask him to make some calls. He owes me a favor and says he'll get to work on this right away.

Scarlett and I spend a quiet night eating takeout food in front of the small television. She insists on having me translate instead of putting up English captions. The shows are dumb, not entertaining, but it feels like the right kind of night for us. There is a normalcy to it that I had not realized I wanted so badly. I see now that I could have this with her. We could be part of each other's lives like this. If she wanted it, too.

I excuse myself to the restroom at some point, realizing with some chagrin that I never really cleaned up after practice. I take a quick shower and allow myself to think while the hot water sluices over my sore muscles. I feel myself softening, with Scarlett in my life. In fact, moving to Las Vegas has made me softer. Not as an athlete, not as a player. But as a man. I am more aware of human emotion, more aware of the value of friendships. I had not really contemplated these things, this evolution, but I see it very clearly now.

I am a big man, but I feel very humbled and very small when I think of the ways I have been changed this year. I suddenly miss my strange friendship with loudmouthed Tyler. And I am all the more in love with Scarlett. More than yesterday, and likely less than tomorrow.

When I emerge from the bathroom, wet and wrapped only in a towel, Scarlett is asleep in the bed we now share. I watch her sleep for a moment, her mouth slightly open. I crawl into bed next to her, naked, and even in sleep she is drawn to me. She turns to face me; her arm draping over my midsection. She stirs slightly, her hand finding my cock, which hardens instantly at her touch.

I pull her closer, settling her body on top of mine, my hands in her hair as I kiss her lightly. Groggy, her eyes open and she gives me a heart-stopping, sleepy smile.

"I thought I was dreaming you," she says.

"It is you that is a dream."

Her pelvis rubs against my bare cock now, the softness of her silk panties an agonizing tease. I want her. Always, I want her, so I slip the soft material to the side and she slides easily on top of me, a soft moan escaping her lips as she takes my cock inside her.

We make love in this dream-like state, her half-asleep, me wired to every touch, every moan, every clench from her. After we are finished and in that post-orgasm state of bliss, she falls asleep again, this time with her limbs twisting with mine, her head on my chest.

I kiss her forehead as I feel my own eyes get heavy and I'm nearly asleep myself when I hear her speak very quietly into the night.

"I know now. I'm sorry I didn't say it before."

"Say what?" My heart starts beating faster as I wait for her to answer me.

"I know now that I fell in love with you, too. That I love you…"

I smile into the darkness.

24

surprises in sochi

Scarlett

Two weeks later.

Viktor has a day off and we're supposed to take a day trip to Sochi to see where he played in the Olympics. I'm dumbfounded when he tells me we'll have to take a plane. Even though Moscow and Sochi are both Russian cities, they're over a thousand miles apart. To drive there would take us something like twenty hours.

"Russia is really big," I state as I look at the map while we await clearance to board the private jet Viktor has arranged for the day.

"Is big, yes," he answers, checking his phone.

"Why are you so distracted?" I ask.

"I am arranging a meeting in Sochi," he says, that familiar frown on his face lit up by the screen of his phone.

"Oh, something I should cover for Crush social media?"

"No," he says quickly.

I'm taken aback by his abrupt tone. What could he be setting up, then? More time with the shady-suit guys who make him pee into a cup once a week? Oh, goody. Just the way I want to spend a tourist day with my boyfriend.

By the time we board the jet, I'm too annoyed to be impressed. We climb on and I toss my stuff into an empty seat, then flop down, putting on my seatbelt and staring out the window.

Viktor stands and stares at me, probably waiting for me to move my bag, but when I don't he just sighs and takes the seat across the aisle.

A pretty, blonde flight attendant in a slim, navy dress tells us the safety features of the plane and offers us something to drink or eat. I ask for a Sprite and she brings it, along with a basket of snacks to choose from, also delivering a beer to Viktor.

"*Pzhalyusta, ostav'te nas v pokoye,*" Viktor growls at the poor woman. I have no idea what he said, but it didn't sound nice.

To her credit, she smiles and gives a short nod. "*Proto nazhmite knopku, yesli vam ponadobitsya,*" she says to him, all professionalism. To me, she switches to English and says, "Push the button if you need me."

She disappears as the plane starts to taxi down the runway. I glare at Viktor, who sips at his beer and looks at his phone, typing another message, to my further-increasing annoyance.

As we get into the air, I finally ask, "What the heck is keeping you so focused on that phone?"

Viktor turns the phone off and tosses it onto the seat next to him, turning his big body toward me. "I told you, is meeting."

"I thought we were spending the day touring Sochi? I wasn't planning on spending the days watching you have meetings with shady dudes," I complain. "What, you have bets to place that can't wait?"

"Why would I travel several thousand kilometers to place betting?" Viktor gives me a hard stare. "That is silly."

He's so earnest with his question that I have to stifle a giggle in response. I want to be annoyed with him. He's been focused on that phone all morning. But he seems genuinely confused about why I'm annoyed.

I sigh dramatically. Viktor unbuckles his safety belt and crosses the divide, tossing my bag to the floor and taking the seat next to me. "I am sorry I have been distracted, but I have something important to do here."

"Do you care to share that important something with me?"

"Not yet," he says, pursing his lips. "Let's find a movie to watch, yes? Or we can join mile-high club?"

"The mile-high club? What is that?"

He chuckles and raises his eyebrows suggestively. "Is the reason I sent attendant away."

It takes me a minute to catch on. "Oh. Oh! Have sex in an airplane?"

He winks in response.

I blush furiously at this. "There are pilots. Like, right on the other side of that door. And the attendant..."

Viktor's hand slides between my legs. His fingers push at my oh-so-sensitive spots through my jeans. My breath hitches and I hear that dark chuckle again.

"She will not come out here unless we call for her," he purrs against my lips.

Needless to say, we spend much of the three-hour flight doing things other than watching a movie.

Immediately after we land, I head straight to the very well-appointed restroom to clean myself up. I swear the flight attendant totally knew what we were doing, even though I was very, very quiet the whole time, and her knowing smile made me blush about ten shades of pink. My whole face is as red as my hair even now, as I brush through my hair, pulling it into a messy braid that falls over one shoulder.

Viktor ushers me straight to a black town car once I emerge. As we ride, Viktor tells me that the Olympic venues have struggled in Sochi since the games. He says that Sochi was a natural choice for the Olympics, as it is a tourist destination already, sitting on the Black Sea with plenty of beaches for a summer crowd to enjoy. In the winter, it is fairly desolate, though, and when we pull up to one of the Olympic venues, I see what he means. There are people milling around with cameras, but all in all, it's pretty much a ghost town.

We wander into the hockey arena and he talks about his time as an Olympic athlete. He has funny stories, and stories that make me cringe. He really was a different man when the Winter Games were held here. I tell him so and ask him if he feels the same.

He shoves his hands into the pockets of his jeans and bows his head. "I was just thinking this the other night, Scarlett. I am different than just a year ago, really. Las Vegas has changed me. *You* have changed me."

"Me?" I ask incredulously.

"You. Realizing I could have hockey and love both. And have friends like loudmouth Tyler to hang out with. I was very concentrated on hockey and nothing else. I am realizing I missed so much by focusing too hard on sport. A life with no love or friendships is not much life at all."

I bite my bottom lip and look up at him. "No, it isn't, I agree."

He gives me what I would consider a shy smile. My man is so freaking sexy...and sweet. I told him I knew I loved him when I was sleepy and sex sated. But I also know that I meant it. And hearing him use the word again makes my heart leap.

"You know, you've changed me too, Viktor."

"In a good way I hope," he says quietly as he pulls me into his arms and just holds me close against his solid warmth.

"Most definitely, and in so many ways. You made this trip possible for me and helped me to find the confidence to believe in myself and to learn that I am going to be okay. I can move forward now with my life and let go of all the bad things in my past. For that help, I will always be so grateful to you. You helped me to find love again too—"

I don't get to finish my speech because the man I love—who also loves me—is kissing me senseless out in the open at the very public Sochi Olympic village. Neither of us care a bit.

Somehow, seeing Stephen's face on that screen allowed me some strange closure that I didn't even realize I needed. The biggest thing is knowing that there aren't men out there ready to bust down my door ready to finish what was started two years ago. The knowledge nobody is going to take my money or blood (or worse) as payment for my father's debts— has totally freed me. And Viktor is the person who made that knowledge possible.

WE DON'T STAY LONG in the Olympic park. Instead, we head down to the tourist areas near the beach to get lunch. Viktor says he wants to take me to a traditional Russian restaurant and ushers me into a darkly lit place that smells of meat and cabbage and bread. It makes my stomach grumble. Viktor says something in Russian to the hostess, and she nods, beckoning us through the main seating area, and into a private dining room.

Only we're not the only people here. No. There is a man. He has thick, brownish-red hair and his eyes...they're my eyes.

The word that comes out of my mouth is barely a whisper. "Dad?"

Mike Woods was my world growing up. He was the life of the party, loud and funny with eyes that were alight with mischief. It's part of the reason he so easily slid into the party scene, his wide smile always a fixture at the card tables. He was a showman, always working an angle, always trying to dazzle people with jokes and stories. He always had beautiful women trying to get his attention.

And yes, my father often took me with him to card games. We didn't do normal things together, like go to the park or travel to the beach. No, a fun father-daughter night for us was getting dressed to the nines and watching a Vegas show, having a big, buffet dinner, and then heading to an underground card game on the Strip somewhere. Me, a tiny little ghost being "babysat" by one of the hostesses away in the background coloring or watching TV while he cleaned up against opponents who took his affable nature for granted.

Mike Woods was a shark, and I loved him. I savored every minute I had with him.

My mother got sick when I was six. She had bone cancer and while I have photos of her, red-haired like me, I don't really remember her as a healthy, vibrant young mom. My father's sister, Aunt Jodie, raised me. My dad gave her custody after my mom's death when I was twelve, so I lived with her and my two older cousins, Matt and Rob. Aunt Jodie and the boys provided a pretty normal childhood, but it was in stark juxtaposition to the every-other-weekend visits I had with my dad after Mom died.

When I graduated high school, Stephen and I had already met through poker via my dad, and soon he moved to Vegas. The three of us—Stephen, my dad, and I—were like peas in a pod at first. But Stephen got moodier, darker. His addiction to gambling grew along with his addiction to pills. And my dad grew nervous and jittery. Sometimes I'd find the two of them whispering, both of them frantic until they saw me, when they would straighten up, smile, and act like nothing was wrong. I was so naïve, so blind, that I had no idea that they would both be missing from my life in only a couple of short years.

So now I'm standing in a restaurant in Russia, half a world away from that life, and I'm seeing my father sitting with a bowl of borscht in front of him. He stands and holds his arms out. He looks fit and slick in a dark suit.

"Baby girl," he says, and there are tears in his eyes.

I don't even realize Viktor is holding my hand, but I look to him for guidance. For an explanation.

"I told you we would find him," Viktor says.

I turn back to my dad, mouth hanging open like a fish. My father steps closer and I'm being pulled into his hug. Feeling him, solid and real, I let myself fall apart. Tears flow down my cheeks and I pull away, worried I'll mark his nice suit. I feel like a little girl again, somehow. It's a very strange sensation.

"Dad…how are you here? Why are you here?"

He gestures for us to sit down, so we do. I can't stop my knee from bopping up and down, nervous energy coursing through my body as I wait for an excuse, a story, an apology, anything.

He smiles at me then nods at Viktor. "So, this big guy's your boyfriend, I assume?"

"Yes," Viktor interrupts forcefully. "I am."

My dad holds out a hand and says, "Mike Woods."

Viktor shakes his hand. "Viktor Demoskev."

"Oh, I know exactly who you are. The Mad Russian—Demon Enforcer—one big, scary, solid sonofabitch. Doesn't let a puck go by without a fight."

"You are following hockey?" Viktor asks him.

"More than just following," my dad says, looking at me. "But let me talk with my daughter for a minute before we get to that."

He turns to me, takes both of my hands in his over the top of the table. "My sweet Scarlett. Oh, what a beautiful, young woman you've become. It pains me that I haven't been able to write or call."

"I thought you were dead." And something in my heart breaks a little at having to say the words. I was always afraid to say them out loud, because if I did it would make it true.

"I know, princess. I know, and that wasn't fair at all, but it was safe. I needed you to be safe, and that meant you couldn't know anything."

"Have you had someone watching me all this time, Dad?"

He nods once, his lips in a tight line for just a moment before a familiar lightness returns to his face. "I had to know you were safe. Princess, I had all kinds of issues. Tax evasion being the biggest one. That was brewing even back when your mama died. Her hospital bills were mounting, we were in debt, and I started playing just to make ends meet. But the allure of it was strong and it became a lifestyle. And the lines of right and wrong blurred pretty badly."

"But you just...left," I say. At first my voice is soft, quiet, but I feel an unchained rage fermenting as I let it out, my voice getting stronger. "You just disappeared. I was assaulted by thugs and then I lost Stephen. I was so alone, Dad. I was in the hospital when he died. It turns out he died for *you*. So you and I could be happy and free of all of this crap, still you were gone."

"Honey, you have to believe I tried to do what was right for you. Always. Having you stay with your aunt

Jodie? It was because I knew this life wouldn't be for you. Wasn't right for a little girl. I wanted to give you a chance to have just a normal life. No gambling. No casinos. No bookies."

"But you pulled me into it," I say accusingly. "You made it feel special, like it was our place together. And then with Stephen…"

My voice breaks at his name. I pull my hands away from my father and scoot my chair closer to Viktor. He puts his arm around my shoulder and the weight of it grounds me, reminds me that this is a public place, that I need to calm down. I need to take a deep breath.

"Why did you involve him in all of this?" I ask once the storm cloud had lifted.

"That kid was a born-for-numbers genius." His tone is unapologetic. "He was gifted in math, Scarlett. Gifted. And he loved the game. He was like Rain Man, though certainly prettier and easier to talk to. He ran with it. I tried to slow him down, but he caught fire. The World Series, that was crazy. And he offered to help. He knew I had tax debt. He knew I was in a rat hole, so we came up with a plan. I was going to disappear, come here, start over in legitimate business. Then, once my debts were paid, we were all going to live here, together."

"That's all news to me," I say sourly.

"I know." His face falls from its usual, jovial mask. When I meet his gaze, he looks…haunted. "I didn't mean for Stephen to take the fall for this. I didn't mean to leave you all alone."

Viktor, who has been quiet through all of this, leans forward in his chair. It's a simple action, but the meaning is not lost. He is my protector now. I am not alone anymore.

"What happened with Stephen?" I ask. "Why the drugs? Why were the Russians after him? They came after me, Dad. I ended up in the hospital because of all of this."

My dad takes a deep breath and then lets it out as he sits back in his chair. He runs his palms all over his face. "Stephen started firing big money. He played the percentages and had every overlay in his favor. I don't really know how much you truly understand about making bets and playing sports, but he was amazing at it. Football, basketball, fighting, horses. He understood the odds, knew how to hedge his bets, when to parlay. He did everything right, and I'm not overstating it when I say he was a pure genius. His genius helped me get out, get over here, get hidden. It helped me build a business and pay off debts really quickly. But then...he just went on an epic cold streak. The winning stopped. The money stopped. And I was here. I couldn't do much to help him from so far away. He got obsessed with turning the tides, but—"

"Did someone you know have him killed?"

"No, honey, never. Stephen was working a lot of bookies. Our guys understood who he was, what he could do. They were willing to wait for things to tick upward. But I know other collectors came calling with threats a few times."

"Dad, he was up sometimes twenty hours a day, obsessed with the bets and the games. He was using crazy amounts of drugs to stay functional. It was…"

I let out a noise that's somewhere between a strangled cry and a growl.

"What did the police say after he died?" my father asks.

"They said suicide. Too much speed in his system. His heart gave out. But Dad, he wasn't suicidal. I may have been naïve to everything going on, but I know that about him. I know he loved me. He loved you. He wouldn't have killed himself. And in the video… he left a video telling me you were alive here in Russia. I just got it recently."

"I know about the video, princess. I sent one of the guys to make sure it was placed into your hands as soon as I saw you were posting from Russia."

"You knew I was here?" my question is high-pitched and sounds hysterical

"You knew I had someone watching, honey." His answer is so simple, so concise. He takes a sip from his water glass.

"They were knocking on the doors in the video, Dad. He seemed worried. You saw."

"And the police told you his heart gave out," Dad says. He looks genuinely sad now, all of his showman glow gone. "He wasn't murdered, sweet pea. Those guys were just wanting to check and make sure he was still working to make them money. They were well aware of the drug use and were trying to keep him alive. But addiction is brutal that way... He just... his body just could not handle all the stress he put on himself. And I feel responsible every day for it. I owed that kid. He deserved better. You deserved better. I'll never forgive myself for how things went down."

"So...you made it easy for Viktor to find you, then?" I ask. "For what? To get me to tell you I forgive you?"

"I hope you'll forgive me, yes." His shoulders slump a little but then he straightens himself and looks me right in the eye. "I'm so sorry, Scarlett. So sorry for everything that happened and for hurting you for even one minute. But things are different now. And you're this amazing woman with a great job and a tank of a boyfriend. This guy is a hockey legend over here, did you know that?"

Viktor snorts at this.

"And you're supposed to be all legit now?" I ask, disdain and disbelief coloring my tone. "Why are you here, Dad? What the hell are you doing in Russia of all places?"

He winces a little at the sharpness of my question. I realize, in the moment, the shine of my dad has worn off. I didn't understand everything that was going on with him and Stephen. I was so young, only eighteen when everything started. I knew very little about the world. But now…now I realize I can survive on my own. I've been working and paying my own bills. I've decided when and who and how in all aspects of my life. I think my dad sees that now, too.

"I know you feel abandoned and betrayed," he begins. When I start to shoot back a biting response, he raises his hands in what looks like surrender and keeps speaking. "I love you. Nothing about that has changed. I've always loved you. Always tried to protect you. I know I messed up, in so many ways, but here you are now. Safe. Successful. Smart. I must have done some things right, didn't I?"

I think about this for a moment and then give a nod. When I think about my father, I have really only good memories. It's only been the last few years, the not knowing, Stephen's death, that makes me feel so angry and confused.

"Vlad says your father is very successful here," Viktor says quietly in my ear. "I think he tells truth to you."

My father nods. "It wasn't easy here at first. They have ways of keeping you on the straight and narrow over here. But I had a financial rebirth. I used my skills to build a brand. I learned the sport of hockey and worked on a business plan, and now I'm majority owner of a Russian Junior Hockey League minor team that feeds players directly into the KHL. It's a real career. Real money. And I'm free of my old debts."

"Scarlett, he owns *Salavat Yulaev*. This is the team

I played for right before I went pro. Is hard to believe, but your father is a true hockey businessman now," Viktor informs me.

This is so much information. I thought we were coming here to see the sights, not reconnect with the past three years of my life. I turn to Viktor, feeling the crease form between my eyes, feeling the panic rising as I process everything I've heard today.

Viktor pulls me to face him. His forehead meets mine and he talks in a low voice as he holds my shaking hands. "This is the chance for you to be free, my love. Is way for you to let go of past and move forward. Las Vegas was my chance. This is yours, yes?"

"I've been carrying this weight for so long," I say in a small voice.

"I know. I know, Scarlett. You are strong. Brave. You are not alone now, though. Not anymore."

All the anger seems to dissipate, then, leaving behind a mixture of sadness and hope and forgiveness. He's right. I'm not alone. I have him. My dad, who I love no matter what, is alive. Stephen was trying to help him, trying to do something good with a bad habit. I can let this go. I can choose to move on. With Viktor. And once I embrace this new revelation, I feel a lightness that I haven't felt at all in my adult years.

"I love you."

His big hand is suddenly on the back of my neck, his lips on mine. The kiss is quick, fierce. It shoots through my body like rocket fuel, strengthening me.

I turn back to my dad and realize it's time to tell him I forgive him. "I love you too, Dad, and I forgive you. I just want my daddy back in my life somehow and however that happens I will just have to have an open mind about it."

After another round of hugs, we talk for a while about my job with the Crush, and about how Viktor and I met. He tells me again how proud he is of me. Then he pulls up a web page for the team he owns.

"So I've been thinking," Dad says. "See this dinosaur of a site? It needs a facelift. And we need some social media, though the rules here are different than they are in the US, I know we could really use someone like you. You could stay here, work with me. Help me build this thing even further."

"Are you offering me a...job?"

He smiles. "Yes, that's exactly what I'm doing. You've got the chops. The experience. I can use you. And we can get to know each other again."

I let out a funny little laugh. I'm not sure what I'm feeling, but it isn't the desire to stay in Russia with my dad. I stand and he stands, and then I pull him into a tight hug. "Dad, I love you. I'm relieved you're okay. I'm glad things are better for you. But my life is back in Vegas right now. I'm doing really well, and I love working for the Crush. And, you know, there's a player I have my eye on."

Viktor's big form appears right behind me, his hand at the small of my back.

"Vik," my dad says, salesman tone all over whatever he's about to say next. "You could coach. Hang up those skates and help the next generation. Bring my daughter back to me?"

Viktor turns to me and takes my cheeks in his big but ever gentle hands. "You choose me over this possible career...with your papa, Scarlett?" I have never seen Viktor look so vulnerable yet confident, and then it comes to me. He was rejected many years ago. The girl he thought loved him chose her career over him. *And I will never make that mistake.* "Yes, Viktor. I choose you." His eyes roam between mine and then the smile that overcomes his face is his most brilliant yet. *God, I love this man.* He turns back to my dad.

"Thank you, but no. Your daughter is my home. In Las Vegas."

As I hug my father one more time, he tells me how much he loves me. How sorry he is. And I tell him this is the last time he has to apologize. We're square. I'm okay.

And I am.

25

new season - new beginnings

October
Season opener.

I look down at the sweet little ring that nestles perfectly on my right ring finger. It's got several small, gold leaves that intertwine, small diamonds sparkling through the vines and leaves. Viktor gave it to me as soon as we returned from Russia. He looked a little nervous when he pulled out the box, which made me nervous too. Even though we've both acknowledged we love each other, I'm not sure I'm ready for more just yet. He bought a gorgeous house in Summerlin and asked me to move in. Even though living together felt too soon, I couldn't turn him down. He's become a part of me.

This ring is a promise. That's what he said. He told me it reminded him of the curves of my body, of the waves in my hair, of the way our limbs intertwined after we made love.

Right? I was swooning after that, too. He probably could have asked me to move to Mars and I would have followed him. I love how Viktor can move our relationship forward to a stronger place without me feeling pushed faster than what's comfortable for me. He gets me. It's strange but I realize he always has. From the very first, Viktor seemed to accept and understand me...and be satisfied with what I had to offer him. Always content to wait for me and be the steady and reliable man by my side. Something I never really had growing up but now realize I can't live without. I need him and love him so much...and I believe it's the same for him.

Pam grins from her seat next to me in the Crush owner's box. It's game one of the new season. Our men are back on Vegas ice, where they should be.

"That's a cute little ring," she says with a knowing grin.

"Yep, I like it a lot."

"I'll bet you like the dude who gave it to you even more," she teases.

"Truth, I agree. He's a pretty solid dude."

"Solid," she says, laughing. "That's punny."

"Puns are my side gig. But was that really a pun?"

"I mean, I think it was a pun." Pam makes a funny face at me. "He's a tank of a man. He's pretty solid. You said he was solid. Pun."

I shake my head and say, "I think if it requires

this much discussion, it probably doesn't count as a real pun."

"Well, we'll agree to disagree on this one," she says, grinning. We turn our attention to the action down on the ice. "They look good out there. Focused."

"They do," I agree.

"Viktor's already leading in votes for All-Stars?" she asks.

"Yeah, but it's early in the season," I say. "He could chuck somebody across the ice and be a hated villain again."

"Fickle fans," she says.

"He's still Viktor," I say with a shrug. "He's a softer version of Viktor, at least with me and his teammates, but he's still kind of a ginormous asshole on the ice."

"He has the *Mad Russian Enforcer* brand to uphold," she says, giggling.

"That he does." I focus on my phone for a minute, watching for social media reaction to some of our pre-game promotions.

"I can't believe Viktor found your dad in Sochi," she comments before groaning at a hard check against the ice. "Oooh. I think that was Georg."

"He okay?" I look up and Georg is arguing with the guy from the other team. The ref steps in and Georg skates off in a huff.

"Yeah, he's okay," she says. "Testosterone city down there. I can smell it."

"Be careful. All that testosterone might get you pregnant, Pamela. Keep your legs closed."

She laughs out loud at this. "Good lord. I'd be a terrible parent. Our kid would be totally shortchanged in that department."

"Well, I turned out okay, despite the parent I got," I say. "And Viktor only had to follow the breadcrumbs my dad left. Dad wanted us to find him."

"You seem conflicted about this reunion," she says gently.

"I'm not conflicted. I'm glad. It was good to put all that behind me. And I'm glad he's doing well in Russia with his team. But I'm not daddy's little girl anymore, you know?"

"I get you, friend. I totally get you." Pam puts her hand on my leg and gives it a squeeze before returning to watch the game. It's wonderful having a friend like Pam for support. I am so grateful to have her in my life.

Fiona sits next to me a few minutes later. "I just finished reading your full-length piece on the Russian summer league. I love how you wove Viktor and Georg's backstories in. It was really well done."

"Wow," I say, feeling my eyebrows fly up into my forehead. "That's a really nice compliment, Fiona, thank you."

"I am capable of giving credit where credit is due," she says. She taps her manicured fingernails together. "I wasn't sure it was a great idea to invest in you going over there, but everyone really enjoyed the social media, and the story really ties it together. It's a great off-season piece. Bravo."

"It was a life-changing experience, and I thank you for the opportunity." Even though management knows that Viktor and I are in a relationship and now living together, not one word was said about the dreaded non-fraternization policy by anyone. So we don't mention it either. We both just do our jobs well and go about our business. I am not complaining. *Knock on wood.*

Fiona seems satisfied for the moment, stands up, and heads off to talk to Max Terry. I move to the window to get a few shots of the game from above. Viktor bought me a very nice camera after he saw the shots I got while we were in Russia. I'm giving Sid a run for his money now, I guess, doing some of the team's official photography in addition to my other work.

I'm thinking about going back to school to study photography actually. Still mulling the possibilities, but excited to do something to build on the skills I've been honing here at the Crush. When I look down and see my man on the ice, working hard for his team, I'm doubly grateful for the past year. I feel lucky and happy and strong and independent. And being with Viktor doesn't diminish any of those feelings at all—only enhances it.

26
lovey birdy

Viktor

Scarlett and I sit at a candlelit table in a small restaurant off the Strip. It is quiet here, and I don't get as many requests for photos and autographs as in other, more popular places, so it has become our favorite place to eat.

Yes, I have started to sign autographs and take pictures with fans. I know, it is hard to believe, but Scarlett says it will help me to get more votes for All-Stars, so I have agreed.

"Tyler excited?" she asks. "He got a really nice, three-year contract."

I nod. "As you can imagine, his excitement was very loud and colorfully spoken."

"Well, your excitement is also sometimes very loud and colorfully spoken," Scarlett says wryly.

"Different kind of excitement."

"You have a very dirty sex mouth, Viktor."

"You like my dirty sex mouth," I answer.

She grins, her cheeks turning pink. "I might like it a little."

"A lot," I amend. "I know this because of the way your pussy clenches when I say dirty things to you."

"Geesh," she says, fanning herself with her hand. "No matter that we're in a public place."

"I will take you in the restroom and show you that it is no matter. I will have you any way, anyhow, anywhere."

She looks around, seemingly contemplating this invitation, then gives me a mischievous grin. "While I enjoy our adventurous sexcapades, let's talk about your meeting with Max. What did you guys talk about?"

I spear at my steak as I talk. "We talked about new contract, about bonuses. We talked about what happens if the Crush will win another championship this year."

"Big money, that's what," Scarlett says.

"Yes," I agree. "Many incentives for this year. Agents are doing their jobs well."

"Are you sad you missed the Olympics?" she asks with a cute pout of her pretty lips.

"No," I say. "Was happy to have a break from Olympic play."

"Will you play in Milan for the next one?"

"If my body holds up and my country calls, I will serve in whatever capacity they need me."

"Your body better hold," Scarlett says. "I've got plans for it for a lot of years."

I chuckle at this and wink at her.

"Did you just wink at me, Viktor Demoskev?" She acts mock-shocked. "Are you flirting with me?"

"Always," I say. "I have had an offer to coach youth teams for a few weeks in the summer. You will join me in Russia? My mother and sister want to meet you."

"Beat the Vegas heat? I'm totally there, baby. And I want to meet your family too. I was bummed your mom was away visiting your sister in Germany when we were there last summer."

We have done FaceTime with her, so they know each other a little, but Scarlett and my mother must still meet in person and spend time together to really know one another. I have never cared to bring anyone home to meet my family before Scarlett. "It will be a nice break, yes? After our visit I will help the Crush bring the cup home to Las Vegas where it belongs."

"That's the spirit," she says encouragingly. "But you're so busy with games and travel, how will you find time for me?"

I stand and hold out a hand, pulling her to me. We slow-dance to the soft music in the restaurant, and I do not care who sees us. I love having her close, love feeling her curves against me. I kiss her temple, her jaw, her neck as she sighs in response.

"I will always make time for you. We are lovey-birdy," I say against her sweet lips.

"Lovey-birdy?" With a giggle, she asks, "Do you mean lovey-dovey?"

"Yes, I think that is it. Besides, I need you to make time to recover from passionate lovemaking each day."

We don't stay for dessert. We can barely finish our meals we want each other so badly. When we return to our spacious new home, which is twenty miles from the glittering lights and constant sounds of the Strip, we're both naked before getting five feet into the foyer.

I have her legs around my waist and my cock inside her as we hit the wall of the living room. Her gorgeous breasts are smashed against my chest, my mouth is on her neck as her fingernails dig into my ass.

This is not the first time we have christened this wall. It will not be the first time we fuck on the heavy, wood dining table. It will not be the first time I use my tongue to make her come in our oversized shower.

As the showerheads catch us from three different directions, I fall to my knees, spreading her lips with my fingertips, dipping my tongue inside of her. She moans and pushes her hips toward my face. I slip a finger inside, then two, moving in and out, sucking on her clit, driving her mad. Her legs nearly give out as she clenches, her fingertips pinching at those sweet, tight nipples.

"Come for me, sweet Scarlett," I encourage. "Let me taste you."

Her hips move against my fingers, my mouth and

then...she explodes spectacularly, crying out nonsense that is barely human and definitely not English.

I rise triumphant and pick her up, taking her against the shower wall, fucking her for the third time tonight. I cannot stop wanting her. I cannot stop loving her.

Later, we lie in our very large, new bed, wrapped up in one another. "I like this house," Scarlett comments as a yawn escapes.

"I do also," I say. "Is providing very nice places to fuck."

"It also has a nice, big bed. Bigger than the tiny one in Russia."

"I liked our bed in Russia. Was small but kept you close."

"I liked it too," she says snuggling in tighter to my side.

"This house is close to new practice facility," I say. "That is good."

"That's pragmatic. Proximity to the practice facility is nice, but I was more thinking that this feels like a home. It feels like our place together, you know?"

I do know. And I tell her so in a language that has become very familiar to both of us.

27

i have scarlett fever

Scarlett

March

The Crush is a shoo-in for the playoffs. Work is super busy for me because of the hype. The team is playing strong, and we've had a lot of fun with the social media. I've also started writing feature articles and doing photos for an online magazine that we're producing each month, in addition to preparing a photography installation for a local art gallery that's doing a whole series on sports-themed art.

I'll start taking classes at UNLV in the fall, which is exciting and nerve-wracking. And Viktor is already planning his summer in Russia. He's been asked to play summer league again, but my dad's comment about coaching got him thinking. There is a young protégé, just fourteen years old, whom Viktor has been mentoring all year. They do Skype sessions and exchange videos from the ice. I've covered a lot of it for the Crush, and fans are eating it up. So Viktor's plan is to go to Russia and spend the summer working with this kid, hoping to get him ready for professional play by the time he's sixteen.

The Crush is on a three-day break after a grueling road trip that crossed three states and included six games. As I head home from the office, I pick up some takeout for dinner. It turns out that neither of us is a very good cook, so we are eternally grateful for the food culture in Vegas.

When I get home, I call for Viktor but he doesn't answer. He said he was going to work out and then do a few projects around the house, so I assumed he'd be home.

I slip off my shoes and head upstairs, eager to change into yoga pants and a T-shirt. When I head into our bedroom, I can't help the smile that breaks through at the sight that greets me.

It's pretty amazing.

Viktor lies naked on top of our bed. There are rose petals strewn all over, candles lit, and soft music playing.

"What's all this, my love?"

"I am sick." He gives a fake cough to make his point.

"Sick?" I can't help grinning. "Too much sex?"

"No," he says quickly. "I have Scarlett Fever."

I crack up at this. "Oh, well, that is terrible. How can I help?"

"You can marry me."

Everything stops. My hands freeze over the buttons as I was unbuttoning my blouse. My head tilts to one side. Viktor turns onto his side, his amazingly chiseled body on full display. I did not notice the tiny ring box on the nightstand but I see it there now. I see the champagne chilling in a wine bucket. I see the two flutes awaiting the sweet, bubbly, cheerful drink.

I think he's proposing to me.

"Aren't you supposed to be on one knee, or something?" The words tumble out of my mouth without conscious thought.

He gets off the bed and quickly drops to one knee, the ring box now in his hand. He pops it open and the most amazing, emerald-cut diamond solitaire twinkles at me in the candlelight.

"As you wish," he says, a line he is quoting from *The Princess Bride*. It's one of my favorite movies and I've now made him watch it about, oh, probably fifty times over the past year. "Scarlett, you make me a better man. You are perfect to me, always so perfect. I want nothing more than to call you my wife. *Ty moya rodstvennaya dusha.* You are my soul mate. My life partner. My forever. And even if I never carry another cup around the ice, even if I never wear another medal on the Olympic podium, I will always win. Because I will have you. Will you marry me?"

I'm crying as I fall to my knees in front of him. I have no pants on and my shirt is half unbuttoned. My breath probably smells like the hummus I had for lunch. He's totally naked. But yeah, it's kind of perfect.

"Yes."

He slips the ring onto my left hand and we admire it for a moment.

"It's beautiful and I love it," I whisper. "Thank you."

"I will give you the moon, Scarlett, if you want it. I am forever yours."

"The things you say," I answer, sucking in a big breath.

"You like it."

"I do," I admit.

My shirt is gone in an instant. Then my bra and panties. He helps me to my feet and we pop open the champagne, toasting to our future.

Sweet liquid on his lips, he leans in for a lingering, smoldering kiss that makes my toes curl. It doesn't matter how many times we've made love, how many ways, in how many places. He always makes me feel like this—like the earth has stopped turning, like we're the only two people in the universe.

"How did I get so lucky?" I ask when the need for air breaks our kiss.

"I am the lucky one," he says. "I am a much better man because of you, Red Rocket."

"I still hate that nickname."

"Noted," he says with a chuckle. "I will make it up to you."

"How many times?" I ask coyly.

"As many as it takes."

epilogue

Scarlett

May

We are on a short trip in Sochi on a bye week before the playoffs. Wedding plans are underway and Viktor wants to ask my father for my hand in marriage. I told him it seems backward, since we've been engaged for weeks and, frankly, I don't feel like my dad needs to weigh in on my personal life at this point.

He insists, though, so we've made the trek overseas. Sochi, it turns out, is gorgeous in the springtime, the mountains still capped with snow, a contrast to the vast green hills below. I take a ton of pictures as we travel.

I've been feeling a little under the weather since we left Vegas, so I actually bow out of our first dinner on the ground that evening. Viktor will meet my father and ask for my hand, so I think it's probably good for them to get some time alone together.

Pam FaceTimes me as I wander the streets, trying to shake off the nausea, which I'm attributing to jet lag.

"What's up, girlie?" she asks.

"Just got in. Viktor's off to meet my dad. I'm not feeling super awesome, so I'm taking a walk, trying to get some air."

"Hmmm, do you think it was something you ate?"

"Not sure," I say with a shrug.

"Period?" she guesses again.

I ponder this. "Now that I think about it, I am late with my period," I share with Pam, but quickly shake it off. "Things have been really hectic at work...I mean, you know. Playoffs coming and all."

"You pregnant, friend?" she asks.

"I don't—" Finishing my sentence goes out the window as I face the fact that Viktor and I are just not very careful most of the time. "It's possible," I admit in a small voice.

"Okay then...well, I think you best go find the Russian version of CVS."

AFTER PAM'S suggestion I promptly burst into tears. Pregnant? Could I be pregnant with Viktor's child?

Yes, you know it's totally possible.

So many emotions fly through me all in an instant that I kind of freak right on out in the middle of a public street in Sochi. Thank God for Pam. Not only did she talk me down from the proverbial ledge, but she told me it was all going to be okay. She reminded me how much Viktor loved me and how much I love him, and told me that she knew he would be happy about a baby if it was true. And she did all of it via FaceTime while I made my way to the first pharmacy I could find. She even stayed on the line and helped me select a few different kinds of tests from the shelves, and wouldn't let me hang up until I assured her I was okay. She's good, that Pam. After many virtual hugs and kisses, plus my solemn promise to get back to her with the results, we finally say goodbye.

I book it back to our hotel room with my three newly purchased pregnancy tests as fast as my legs can take me.

And twenty minutes later, sure enough, there are double lines on all of them.

I am pregnant.

WHEN I HEAR Viktor's key fumble in the lock a few hours later, I don't know what to do with myself. He's humming, a little drunk, as he sort of tumbles into the room.

His eyes light up when he sees me. Kicking the door closed, he beelines for me, pulling me in for a sloppy kiss.

"I take it my dad said yes." I laugh.

"Yes, and then some. We drank much vodka to celebrate."

"I can tell."

"You want a drink?" he asks cheerfully. "We can celebrate also. Are you feeling much better after resting?"

"I do not want a drink."

He pulls back to scrutinize me. My tone was weird and he caught it, even in his adorable inebriated state.

"Why?" He asks the question slowly.

"I won't be drinking for, oh, maybe nine months or more," I answer, the implication heavy in my voice.

"Nine months?" He looks confused.

"Yep. Nine months."

He stares at me and I see the moment he gets it. His eyes go wide.

"You are—we are?"

"We're having a baby, my love."

I have never seen a man as big as Viktor Demoskev faint. His body just gives out and he goes down to the floor. Thankfully, there is no furniture nearby, so the fall is fairly graceful, under the circumstances. He made a remarkably soft landing, which was a good thing since I had zero chance of keeping him upright. The laws of gravity and all.

A moment later, he sits up from where I'm kneeling next to him and I can't help but giggle at the spectacle. It's probably nervous laughter on my part, really, but still…

"Are you okay?"

"From the fall or the news?" he asks, rubbing the back of his head.

"Both?"

"I am okay," he says firmly. I bite my lip and he looks me straight in the eyes, suddenly sober for a moment. He puts his fingers under my chin and kisses me for good measure. "We made baby."

"We did. We made a baby."

"Well, then we have two things to celebrate," Viktor announces as he gets up from the floor. He wastes no time before scooping me up and whisking me to the bed.

"Told you I can't drink."

"There are other ways to celebrate," he says, grinning wickedly.

Viktor pulls my shirt over my head and spends a long time kissing at my very tender breasts. He is sweet and soft with his mouth and tongue, and I almost come just from the attention he pays there. He kisses my belly almost reverently before moving up to my neck and ears and jaw and chin. There is no part of me from the waist up that does not receive his love and attention, and he asks nothing in return. Instead, he finds new and creative ways to make me clench with orgasm, and I'm shocked by what he can do to me, even after nearly a year together.

When I pull away my pajama bottoms, he places a simple kiss on my stomach before rolling over to his back, an invitation to play. I spend the same amount of time and care with his body, kissing all of him, touching him, making him harder. I take him in my mouth, making sure that we don't break eye contact while my mouth and tongue tease his lovely cock.

I align my whole body with his, savoring the feeling of being skin to skin with him. Just the act of touching him, teasing him, makes me come again, and I slip on top while I clench uncontrollably around him.

"My God, Scarlett," he growls.

"Being pregnant apparently makes my body do weird things," I tell him through another shudder of pleasure.

"Well, we'll have to keep making you pregnant then," he says.

"Babies for days." I'm still coming as I ride him.

"Babies for days," he repeats, a wide smile brightening his handsome face.

"I live for that smile," I say. "Also, I can't stop coming."

"I live for you," he says. "And now our little family. And I don't want you to."

As we explore each other with this love and

excitement in our hearts, I realize he is right. There is more than one way to celebrate.

And more than one chance at love.

For that, I am very grateful.

Once upon a time a big Russian hockey player scowled at me for taking his picture.

It was the best thing that's ever happened to me.

my thoughts about...

afterword

Extensive creative license was applied in portraying some elements of NHL games, fan events and awards, that would ***not happen in real life***. I did this intentionally to create a more enjoyable reading experience within the storyline. These stories have been carefully crafted for your reading pleasure and in no way meant to be a true and accurate representation of NHL best practices and/or official rules currently or in the past.

Hockey Romance F-I-C-T-I-O-N all the way!!!

vegas crush by trope

All books in the **VEGAS CRUSH** series are *STANDALONES* existing in a connected world centering around a Las Vegas ice-hockey team. You can read them out of order if you wish and everything will still make sense with only minor spoilers. I've made a list of tropes for you here.

CRUSHED

BOOK 1

Forbidden, Reformed "Player", Ukrainian/American Hero, Good Girl Heroine, Office Romance, Love in the Workplace, He Falls First, Sports Romance, Team Captain, Social Media Manager, Risking it All for Love, Band of Brothers

BOOK 2

Bad Boy Russian Hero, Virgin Heroine, Damaged Heroine, Forbidden, Office Romance, Hockey Defenseman, Team Physical Therapist, Love in the Workplace, Band of Brothers, Overcoming Self-Doubt and Addiction, Trust

BOOK 3

Grumpy/Sunshine, Russian Hero, Feisty Red-Haired Heroine, Forbidden, Office Romance, Hockey Defenseman, Public Relations Manager, Love in the Workplace, He Falls First, Brooding Alpha, Opposites Attract, Band of Brothers

BOOK 4

Opposites Attract, Forbidden Romance, Financial Advisor/Client Relationship, Russian/Romanian Hero, Nerdy Young Heroine, Fresh Start in Vegas, Dyslexic Hero, Gentleman Alpha, Good Guy Hero, He Falls First, Age Gap, Vegas Mafia Suspense, Savior Hero, Band of Brothers, Superstar Hockey Centerman

Smoke SHOW

BOOK 5

Friends to Lovers, Teammates Little Sister, Young Virgin Heroine, Russian Heroine, Boston Native, Bad Boy Hero, Forbidden Romance, First Love, Age Gap, Single "Dad" Vibes, Hardscrabble Upbringing, Band of Brothers, Hockey Defenseman, New Adulting, Found Family

The KEEPER

BOOK 6

Enemies to Lovers, Forced Proximity, Love in the Workplace, Neuro-Diverse Hero, French-Canadian Hero, Rock Chick Heroine, Socially Awkward w/ No Filter, Opposites Attract, Instant Attraction, Fish Out of Water, Band of Brothers, Superstar Hockey Goalie, Rockstar Heroine, Brooding Alpha, Guitar Lessons w/ Cute Kids, Personal Growth, Sacrificing for Love

BOOK 7

Surprise Pregnancy, One Night Stand, Forbidden Romance, Love in the Workplace, Boss/Employee, Office Romance, Sneaky Dates, Instant Attraction, Age Gap, Mature Hero, Gentleman Alpha, Love After Divorce, Can't Keep Their Hands off Each Other, Career Milestones, Team General Manager, Team Nutritionist

BOOK 8

Friends With Benefits, Instant Attraction, He Falls First, Brooding Alpha, Superhero Complex, Gentleman Alpha, Damsel in Distress, Knight in Shining Armor, Living up to Father's Legacy, Vegas Mafia Suspense, Comic Book Nerd, Wedding Planner Heroine, Band of Brothers, Finding Your Voice, Parent/Child Relationships

BOOK 9

Age Gap, Secret Crush, Surprise Pregnancy, Shotgun Wedding, Opposites Attract, The Owner's Granddaughter, The Brooding Hockey Player, Forced Proximity, Only 1 Bed, Career Milestones, Forbidden, Old Family Friends, *Neanderthal* Hero, *Heiress* Heroine, Parenthood, Beliefs, Growing Up, Manning Up, Facing Your Demons, Family Legacy

BOOK 10

Christmas Marriage Proposal, No Third-Act Breakup, Proposal Problems, Brooding Hockey Player Hero, Buying a Home, Festive Holidays, Dear Santa Letter, Gentleman Alpha, Building a Legacy, Comic Book Nerd, Wedding Planner Heroine, Team Captain, Band of Brothers, Family Relationships, OTT Romantic Gifts

about the author

BRIT DEMILLE is the alter ego of *NYT* Bestselling author, Raine Miller, having an absolute blast writing books quite different from what she writes as Raine.

Stories about sexy billionaires [millionaires make the cut too] who fall in instalove with young women who may or may not be virgins, and then go on to make adorable babies together are her favorite themes. In addition to the billionaires, hot hockey players are at the top of her list of favorite heroes, along with royals and ex-military bodyguards.

Most important when she writes a story is a happily ever after. But during the actual *writing* of the story, the most important thing is a cup of hot tea with a splash of milk (and don't forget the stash of cherry Jolly Ranchers). A dog or two will likely be in between her and the chair at any given moment, which is very handy, because they are the ones who approve everything she writes.

RAINE MILLER is a #2 *New York Times*, *USA Today*, and *Wall Street Journal* bestselling author since 2012. Before that, she spent two decades teaching kiddos to read—something she's most proud of. These days, writing steamy romance books pretty much fills up the hours...for which she keeps pinching herself to make absolutely sure she's not dreaming.

#Truth

She has a handsome husband, two amazing sons, and two very bouncy Italian greyhounds to keep her busy the rest of the time. Her boys know she writes romance books but gratefully they have zero interest in reading even a single one. *Thank. God.*

When she's not writing she's likely deep into a hockey game cheering on her beloved VEGAS GOLDEN KNIGHTS and dreaming up a new book. The greyhounds are likely to be in her lap while she writes the books or watches hockey—both dogs at the same time of course!

She loves to hear from readers and chat about the characters she's created.

You can connect with Raine on Facebook in her reader group, **Raine Miller Romance Readers.** She pops in to visit most days because it's a super happy place where romance awesomeness abounds day in and day out with the most amazing readers on earth.

> *My readers are the heart and soul of what keeps me writing the words.*

#Truth2

also by raine miller

The BLACKSTONE AFFAIR

NAKED, Part 1

ALL IN, Part 2

EYES WIDE OPEN, Part 3

RARE and PRECIOUS THINGS, Part 4

The ROTHVALE LEGACY

PRICELESS, I

MY LORD, II

BLACKSTONE DYNASTY

FILTHY RICH, I

FILTHY LIES, II

HOCKEY ROMANCE *as Brit DeMille*

CRUSHED, Vegas Crush #1

SIN SHOT, Vegas Crush #2

RED ROCKET, Vegas Crush #3

PUCK MONEY, Vegas Crush #4

SMOKESHOW, Vegas Crush #5

The KEEPER, Vegas Crush #6

LUCKY PUCK, Vegas Crush #7

Mr. HOCKEY, Vegas Crush #8

CLUSTERPUCK, Vegas Crush #9

Mr. HOCKEY's MARRY CHRISTMAS, Vegas Crush #10

CONTEMPORARY ROMANCE

CHERRY GIRL

HUSBAND MATERIAL

LOVELY PINK

HISTORICAL ROMANCE

The MUSE

The PASSION of DARIUS

The UNDOING of a LIBERTINE

Wedding Night Diaries

LORD BLACKWOOD'S VIRGIN

join raine mail

For my newsletter and information on upcoming books and events, you should definitely sign up for Raine Mail. Use the QR code below.

whispers *There's so many freebies in that thing.*

subscribe to Raine Mail